FIGHTING TUESDAYS

Stories by Fourth Year Students from Larkin Community College

Foreword by Roddy Doyle

Introduction by Hugo Hamilton

A Stinging Fly Press Book

Fighting Tuesdays is published in May 2010 in association with Fighting Words
© Individual Authors 2010

Editors: Emily Firetog & Declan Meade

Set in Palatino

Cover Design: www.pcc.ie

Printed by Colour Books, Dublin

The Stinging Fly Press, PO Box 6016, Dublin 8

www.stingingfly.org

Fighting Words, Behan Square, Russell Street, Dublin 1

www.fightingwords.ie

ISBN: 978-1-906539-13-9

The Stinging Fly and Fighting Words gratefully acknowledge funding support from
The Arts Council/An Chomhairle Ealaíon.

Contents

Foreword

Roddy Doyle

I work in the attic. Don't worry, it's properly floored and heated—it's very nice. I can hear traffic, the Dart, sirens, dogs, the occasional child and, most recently, a rooster. I'm alone for hours, and I like it. On the good days I'm not even aware of it. I've been working this way for years, going up to the top of the house, writing two or three pages, coming back down, hanging out the washing, going back up, another two pages, back down to make the coffee, back up for another page. It's my working day and it only occurred to me a few minutes ago as I started to write this, I've never seen another writer at work.

That's one of the reasons I enjoyed Tuesday afternoons, the fighting Tuesdays. Twenty-four young writers sat and wrote the stories in this book, and I watched them. Their frowns and dark concentration, their laughter, their yawns and stretches—what is it about teenagers and their ability to stretch to three or four times their normal length? The way they filled the pages so quickly, and the way some of them discovered that they had to get up and go to the toilet every quarter of an hour. They were new to the job but already writers, with minds that told them to sit still and concentrate and bladders that told them to get up and wander. There were twenty-four minds in the room, and the twenty-four bladders. Luckily, the minds won and we have twenty-four great stories.

The room mentioned above is a place called Fighting Words,

on Russell Street, very near Croke Park. Class 401, a transition year group from Larkin Community College, went there every Tuesday afternoon. I liked watching them arrive. Fighting Words is in off the street, in a courtyard, and the boys and girls would gather at the entrance to the courtyard, the arch. There'd be two of them, then seven, then thirteen, then twenty-four. It reminded me of Hitchcock's film, The Birds. Then, in a sudden friendly rush, they'd arrive at the door and enter.

There were two rules: a. they had to write fiction; and b. the story had to involve a character, or characters, close to their own age. Some got going very quickly, but there were false starts and changes of mind. That was fine. It wasn't an exam or a rush against the clock. Gradually, the pages filled. Names became characters; vague ideas became plots; good ideas became better; bad ideas were dumped. The pages became stories.

My highlight was a Tuesday in January when all the students finished the first drafts of their stories. There was such pride in the room, and smiles that could have pulled us out of the recession. It was one of the days I was glad I wasn't working alone.

I'd like to thank the volunteers who came to Fighting Words every Tuesday afternoon, and Mairéad Byrne of Larkin Community College. Without them—their generosity and experience—there'd be no book.

Introduction
Hugo Hamilton

It's not really a classroom. It's more of a library, with white shelves full of books all around the walls. There's no blackboard or anything like that. Instead, you have a big screen which is connected to a laptop. Somebody is sitting at the laptop with fingers hovering, ready to type up any ideas that might come up. In fact, the room is more like a giant computer terminal where everything that is said out loud appears on the screen.

The students sit in rows of seats like an audience. Girls and boys all mixed together from Larkin Community College Transition Year. They are here to write a book. To make things up and invent their own stories. Anything that comes into their heads. Over the space of a year, they will fill that blank screen in front of them full of words until they have the makings of a book which will then be published.

'What about the movie rights?' somebody remarks from the back.

The teacher is not really a teacher. It happens to be Roddy Doyle and he's more like an instigator, so the jokes are welcome. The place is called Fighting Words, right next to Croke Park, set up to give children and students of all ages a chance to have a crack at writing. Who knows which of them might get the storytelling bug and become the great novelist or crime writer or screenwriter of the future.

Roddy explains the plan and adds a few jokes of his own, good ones. He tells the students how he got the writing bug himself when he once worked in a newspaper office and his job all day was carrying messages from one part of the building to another between the journalists.

'I was a human e-mail,' he says.

And then it's time to get down to business. He stands in front of the screen and asks the students a few questions that might get them thinking out loud. Anything at all to get the creative engines started up. You can't publish a book full of jokes and smart remarks, so he asks them a more serious question. Something personal.

'Is there anything that makes you angry?'

Deep thinking breaks out all over. That gets everyone's mind working. Remembering things you really hate is not all that difficult. Soon enough, the words start appearing on the screen. For a moment, some of them are written across Roddy's forehead until he steps aside.

'I hate getting up early,' says one girl in the front row.

'Why?'

'I just do. I don't see the point in getting up for school.'

'What would you do if you didn't have to get up?'

'Stay in bed all day.'

So there we have a start, a bit of dialogue. Maybe it's the beginnings of a story about a girl who stays in bed all day and wakes up seventy years later as an old woman. There's a story inside everyone waiting to get out.

'Anything else that gets you really angry.'

'Yeah, not getting served in pubs,' comes the next answer.

The student who can't get served a drink because she's under age turns out to have a job in a pub at the weekends where she serves drink herself all night.

'One night this man came into the pub waving a gun around,' she says. 'But he didn't find who he was looking for so he left.'

Could be a big crime thriller in the making or it could be a true reflection of the way things are in the city. Another student talks about a day when he was playing football on the street with his friends and they heard a gunshot some distance away and then saw men running.

'It sounded like somebody clapping his hands.'

So here are the true stories of Dublin coming out, the inner city gangland crime unfolding in words on the screen.

'Anything else, that makes you personally angry?'

'Yeah. When love doesn't work.'

Laughter. The whole room cracks up, giggling and yelping and talking and arguing. The student who said this has left himself wide open to slagging. The girls sitting near him move away a bit. Everybody staring at him like a fish with three heads. But he's managed to touch on something that everybody must be quietly thinking at the back of their heads, only they're afraid to say it. And maybe this is where the real writing begins, when the most embarrassing thing is finally spoken out loud and written down.

Soon the writing group of Larkin students gets settled into their book. Eventually, it will accidentally be called *Fighting Tuesdays*, because that's what somebody says one day and it's not far from the truth. And each week, they fight with the words and struggle with the technical business of writing.

How does dialogue work? They examine how people speak and how that all looks on screen with quotation marks. There is a cast of two. The student who feels that love never works is standing in front of the screen opposite a girl who disagrees with everything he says. They have a funny argument about life and love and where she has been hiding all this time. A spontaneous bit of invented dialogue which ends up with him asking her for a hug, but then she runs off stage, back to her seat.

Suddenly it's all there in words. From the top of the head. Everything they say to each other. And that's how the stories get invented. Simple as that. Week by week, the students sit down at desks in small groups of two and three. There are about a dozen volunteers helping them along the way with structure, with spelling, with dialogue and continuity. The volunteers are mostly writers themselves who have agreed to give their time every Tuesday afternoon for the year.

Some of the students come up with stories right away. Others take their time to fill the pages. One boy leaves the names of his characters blank, because every name he can think of belongs to somebody else's mother, or aunt, or sister and that might get him into trouble with his mates. Every now and again, somebody explodes into laughter because of something he's read in another story. But soon the gaps all get filled in and the stories get written. And this is the result of all that work and fun and talking and concentrating.

It's the true story of a city. It's real Dublin life, seen from the viewpoint of a schoolboy or a schoolgirl. There are stories here about love and football. Love and drugs. About school and bullying and Bebo and Facebook, about trouble at home and teenage pregnancy. About mothers and school principals and hairdressing and more football. All the stuff that is real and part of people's lives and dreams.

'We're going to get lucky tonight,' writes Kevin Cooney. It's a story of boys out on the town after the Junior Cert results come out and they run into some girls in a club who invite them to a party. How a boy forgets to ask a girl her name until she tells him.

Michael Murphy has stretched his imagination to a village in a far away country which is under attack from a monster called Ruthar. One of his characters has a half-moon scar. Two sisters must escape from their village into the forest where they meet a wise old man on their side.

Soccer comes up many times because every boy has the dream of being spotted by a scout and asked to play for one of the top clubs in England. A story written by Robert Courtney tells about such a boy who was picked for Manchester United and says goodbye to his family. But then one day comes the heartbreaking news. Worse than anything imaginable, he is injured and forced to abandon his footballing career.

Carla works part time at a Dublin hairdresser's in Lorna Moran's story, washing the customers' hair and brushing the floor after them. She is beginning to fall in love with a boy called Cian, who is a big football fan. It's all going really well, but then comes the terrifying reality of life being turned upside down by drink and drugs, when Cian falls under the influence of two other boys who are dealing.

> 'I can't believe it, all the times he told me how bad drugs were and how he would never in his life touch them. Like, we're friends since babies... I'm so worried about him. I can't eat or sleep. Oh God, he's gonna kill himself if he doesn't stop.'

The cruel hand of drugs is at the centre of another story by Sean Ray. A drug deal goes badly wrong and the main character Paul ends up in jail. He happens to be a brilliant football player and maybe this might finally be his way out of trouble in the end.

There is an exciting story called 'Hope', written by Dillon Burke, which tells about an escape from an orphanage. Two teenagers plan their escape in a laundry van, hidden among the dirty linen. The cleaning company is called Eazy-Cleanz. And once they make their escape, they stop in a shop to get two rolls with ham, then make a plan to get across on the boat to an uncle living in England.

Kirsty Hogan tells the story of vulnerable girl, the youngest in the family, who ends up being bullied in school.

> 'Her father moved to America when Lucy was just eight years old. She really misses him and would sometimes wonder is he's gone forever or if he will be back.'

All the time as she imagines her father coming home, she looks at other girls around her and wonders how she will turn out. She sees a girl walking down the street in a football kit, an older girl with a bag on her shoulder. A group of teenagers asleep on the footpath who are homeless. How will she turn out in the end herself?

'Ever wonder what teenagers do in school nowadays?' That's the first line from a story by Marian Ivanov. On Spin 103.8 radio, they're giving away two tickets to a Britney Spears concert. Jim falls in love with a new girl in school called Sally, but she has no time for him, so his friend Sam tells him he's wasting his time. 'Listen, you big buffalo, I think you are better off forgetting about her.'

The story ends up with a big fight between Jim and Sam with three hundred schoolchildren as spectators until the principal arrives. The story is called 'When Love Takes Over' and it ends with a happily ever after.

Another school story from Jonathan Moore tells a familiar scene about a schoolboy being accused in the wrong. A window in the gym is smashed with a stone and there are shards of glass over the students. But who really did it?

A young boy named Daniel is the victim of bullying in the schoolyard when the school bully demands his sandwich, then laughs that the crusts have been cut off by his mother. When he arrives home with black eyes, his mother then enrols him in a boxing club so he can learn to defend himself. But there is a further twist in Josh Douglas's story with an even better reason for a boxing career.

A story by John Cooney called 'The Worst Shock Of My Life' begins with the words 'She told me to sit down.' Anyone would want to read on from that first line. '… she started to cry. I said "What's wrong?" Then she said, "I'm pregnant."'

Graham Burke describes the first brush with crime and the law when boys go into a shop after their Junior Cert results come out and one of them loses the head and starts robbing the shop. But the night is rescued when the narrator meets several girls at a dance.

Some of the stories here give a huge insight into everyday social problems, because they are described with such genuine feeling from the inside. 'A Fixed Life' by Melissa Ward describes the life of a girl whose mother and father are always fighting. She wants to leave the house and her friend helps her, offering to put her up with her family for a while. But then, as with all vulnerable girls, she is under threat because drink and drugs are always within easy reach.

Dale Mulgrew writes a sort of up-to-date Dublin version of the Bonnie and Clyde story, with a young couple, Jimmy and Sara, using a black and white BMW in order to carry out their plan to rob a supermarket.

Talk about love going wrong. Here is a story called 'Sunshine Rise' where Desislava Baramova describes two girls trying to catch the attention of boys at school. When one of them meets a new boy who gives her his number, she discovers that he is really after another girl in her class. So then a fight breaks out between the girls and everything goes downhill.

Natalina Marcella describes teenagers making connections in her story called 'Friendship'. In the Barcode nightclub, girls are pushing each other into fellas they fancy. But that's not the way love works either. They get invited back to a free gaff and after all this looking for romance, the girls find it only causes them to lose a good friendship among themselves.

Two girls are in a big room with a man in uniform at a desk in front of them, staring at them as he takes in a deep breath.

'What did you think you were doing? Thought yous were funny? Mad? Or were ya just not thinking?' He says to them in a story which is entitled 'Chase The Cake,' by Rebecca Heary.

The girls are in deep trouble and there is no way out of it. But when the man is suddenly called away, they decide to make a run for it. As they are followed they even have time to wave at the man in pursuit.

Amanda Miller has come up with a haunting ghost story called 'Crossing Over'. On holidays in a hotel in Italy after finishing their Leaving Cert exams, two girls encounter a figure from the world beyond death wandering in and out of their company. '"Taylor! stop it. You're scaring me," said Laura.' The apparition reveals itself again later on in Room 220 as a young woman in a white flowing dress, a bride who did not survive her own wedding day. But why? They must step into the other world to resolve the mystery of her death.

It's great the way the authentic Dublin dialogue comes out effortlessly in many of these stories. Words like 'alright' are often left in their natural pronunciation as 'awri', adding so much more reality to the voices of the characters in the stories. Cody Wheelock has an ear for the language and we get the phonetic reality of young people on a drinking binge with the random violence told in their own words.

> **Jocelyn:** (*running up the stairs*) Yeh wanna see what's after happening! This dope at the Finglas bus stop goes, 'He'or, youngone, do ya remember me? 'Cause if ya don't ya remember me fella 'cause ya wer with em!' So I said 'No, I don't remember, but you'll remember me,' and I swung out of her. She was in an awful state, God love the poor creature.

In a story called 'Football First?' the real obsession with soccer success is taken apart by Adrian Rafferty. A young boy named Thomas Naysmith gets a contract with Coventry City. He promises to buy his mother a white BMW when he's famous and wealthy. But one night when he is caught drinking by the manager, he gets a call with bad news from his mother and flies straight home to discover that there are more important things in life than football.

Another football story turns misfortune into a happy ending in Artur Vorobjov's story about a boy who gets the call but then breaks his leg. 'The injury is very bad; the bone has come through the skin.' He spends weeks on crutches, then goes to the see the manager. He wants to be included in an important final, so he can't wait for the doctor to take the plaster off so he can get back to training.

With all these stories about football, discussions keep breaking out about the principle of fair play. It's around the time that Thierry Henry handled the ball in the vital match that put Ireland out of the World Cup. So there is a real background to all the soccer fables. Carlos Donovan describes how a player decides to injure another player deliberately with a cruel tackle which sees him being carried off the pitch on a stretcher. A scout for a top English club then signs up the player who committed the foul, because he cannot use an injured player, naturally. It's a serious story which brings up everything there is to be said about fair play and ethics in football.

Carina Tkachova has found inventive ways of telling a tense

romance story set around school in her story called 'Escape Me.' The title alone suggests the playful way that she makes use of language, by turning a noun into a verb and turning a wish into action. She matches all the twists and turns, all the jealousies and angst and dashes expectations of a teenage love story, with a prose style which becomes entirely her own. 'As a tear of condensation rolled down the window, the bus stopped.'

Carina then goes on to develop her drama around love and loneliness in a young girl's mind, writing it out in a log of her life, including the most up-to-date form of communication that exists right now, the text message. 'Hey hun! Miss ya lyk hell): cnt wait till 2nait its gonna b gas! (; I wil giv ya mii flower dress I kno yew luff mii xxx.'

But the story was always heading towards a tragic end. Right from the beginning there are subtle hints of blood and milk intermingling. And towards the end a crash of blood and pearls and shards of glass. What is happening to this young girl and why does her life come to such a tragic end?

And finally, a heartbreaking story written by Ashleigh Eyre about a girl who is caught in the downwards spin of a life on drugs. 'A woman I know a long time now once had a very bad drug addiction.' So the story begins. And you can't help wanting to know what will happen to Shelly and her three children. It's the helpless story of a mother on drugs, trying to rescue herself. She tries to get her life back, but even though she is promised an apartment, her hopes are dashed when she is told at the last minute that she won't get the keys. 'She could do with a break.'

The stories in this book all have a real punch because they are all written from the heart. They are the honest view of life from the inside, written by a group of Dublin students who are describing the world as it is today. It was fun to watch them get there, from the first day the words started lashing up onto the screen right up to the final product. Fair play to them for carrying it through and fair play to the volunteers who cheered them on along the way.

FIGHTING TUESDAYS

Sunshine Rise
Desislava Baramova

When I woke up in the morning, too many things were going through my mind. What was going to happen? Was I going to see him again? I got dressed, put some make-up on and walked out. The twenty minutes on the bus seemed like an eternity. My phone vibrated. I had a new text. It was my friend Julie. It said: First day in skull :O kill me! Hah just kidding girlfriend :P wer u?

We met at the shop beside our school and we walked in the Larkin gates together. And here they came. Keith and his friends were just in front of us. Without even saying a word they walked by us.

We went to the girls' toilet, that was the only place where boys haven't invaded our space yet. And talking about boys... I was shocked, I had no idea I was going to react like this. I thought it was over and I was not going to think about him anymore but... I guess I was wrong.

Keith was a shy guy. He never expressed his feelings. He was such a nice boy though: brown long hair, blue eyes, sexy freckles. He always made me laugh in class. Keith and I had always kinda been only friends and that was it. I had always been mad about him. There was something about his eyes that made me go crazy that day.

We walked into class and as usual Julie decided to sit behind the boys.

*

The next days in school seemed to go pretty well. We were all having fun and trying to enjoy the year. It was a completely new class and Julie was the only one still in it since last year. We had gotten to know each other really well and I opened up a lot with her. We also went through ups and downs, and there was always something or someone trying to break us apart but the friendship we had was really strong.

Julie was a smart girl but not really open to the world. She was very kind to people and that's why everybody enjoyed her company. When we were alone I saw Julie in a different light, she showed me the real her. I was lucky to have a friend like her. The only weakness she had was Chris. Since she came to this school she had fallen in love with him. I had always been there for her when he made her cry and I knew that one day she would be there for me when I needed to cry. We were both really excited about this new school year and the surprises it would have in store for us.

The day of the Junior Cert results: I was nervous. I didn't know how it was going to go. It was 10.15 and we were in class. The door opened and Mr Brown told us to be in the atrium in ten minutes. The moment of truth. They gave us an envelope. I was scared to open it, but I did and I couldn't believe what I was seeing. I didn't expect to do that well. We were definitely going to party that night.

We met at half seven in front of the club Barcode.

'Alright, chicken?' said Susan to me, 'I love your dress. It matches your blonde hair perfectly. Where did you get it?'

'Oh thanks, River Island.' I could not concentrate. I was looking around to see if anyone had arrived. Keith wasn't there but I was convinced he was coming. Maybe he was late. I had to stop thinking about him and just have fun. It was my Junior Night.

The girls and I were dancing when these gorgeous boys came over and started dancing with us. They were so cute that I can't even describe them. One of them especially attracted my attention.

He was tall with blonde hair and green eyes. We started dancing together. He broke the ice:

'So, are you enjoying your night?'

'Yeah, I'd say so,' I answered, looking deep into his eyes.

'Good, good. Looking for anything in particular?'

'What's that supposed to mean?'

'Everybody is looking for love. Ain't that the reason you're at this club?'

'Hah yeah, especially if I get the opportunity to get to know fellas like you.'

'Excellent. Instead of talking, let me demonstrate.'

He moved in for a kiss. My heart started beating faster and faster. With his arms around me I felt secure. Then we met. It was the longest kiss ever until Julie started pulling me.

'What you pulling me for?' I said. 'Don't you see I'm busy?'

'Look, I'm really sorry for interrupting you, Ashleigh, but I can't find Jessica,' she said.

Before I went looking for my friend, I turned around and said:

'I'm sorry, I have to go. One of my friends is missing. I enjoyed talking to you.'

'Oh sure,' he said, disappointed.

I was just walking away when he pulled me back.

'Wait! I'll leave you my number, just in case.' And he winked at me. 'My name is Sean by the way.'

I smiled. 'And I'm Ashleigh.'

'Come on, Ash. You coming or what?' Julie screamed.

'I am! You wanna calm down. I just got the opportunity to meet such a sweetheart, and if it wasn't for you I could have still been talking to Sean.'

'Who?'

'The boy you just saw me with. Are you even listening to me?'

'Yeah, yeah, that one... What about Keith?' Julie answered.

'Eh, Keith who?'

'Eh, hello? The boy you were crazy 'bout until you saw that Sean fella.'

'Well after what just happened I'm not really interested in him anymore. Come on, after all, I got Sean's number. It's not the end of the story.' I said with a big smile on my face.

'I wish I was like you…' she said sadly.

'What do you mean?'

'I mean that I hope one day I see a nice boy and I totally forget about Chris,' she said.

Chris was Keith's friend and he was part of the 'posh gang' as we used to call them. He was a player and somehow he made them good girls go bad for the night and didn't even remember their names next day, or he just chose to do that. With Julie the case was different. He didn't play with her, he just ignored her because she was not the girl that would satisfy his needs.

'Ah, you will one day. Trust me.' I said.

'Yeah. Let's go.'

We went outside, where Jessica was with Sarah and they were in the company of three boys. Getting closer I realised one of them was Sean.

'Where the hell were you?' I said to Jessica.

'Just here outside, getting some fresh air and waiting for you guys. Why, what's wrong?'

'We've been looking for you everywhere.'

While clearing his throat, Sean said: 'Well, we'll be going now. See you, girls. See you, Ashleigh.'

The next day in school I tried to talk to Jessica but I preferred to wait until she and I were on our own.

The first class, maths, was boring as usual, and the second, science, was even worse. I wasn't listening to a word of what the teacher said. It was something about recycling but I didn't really know what.

Julie asked me: 'What's wrong with you today?'

'Who, me? Nothing… I'm just tired.'

'I'd say quite more than tired. You usually never close your mouth during this class.'

'I know…'

At break time I saw Jessica around the music corner and Julie and I went over.

'Hiya,' Julie said.

'Hello,' Jessica said.

'Awh, I'll be right back. I just need to ask Becky bout the geography homework,' said Julie.

'OK,' I said.

The moment was perfect to talk 'bout the previous night.

'So, Jess, I saw you talking to these lads last night outside Barcode, do you know them?'

'One of them was my cousin Graham, so he decided to introduce me to his friend, Sean. They just live across the road from each other.'

'I didn't know your cousin was there,' I said.

'Neither did I, but Sean convinced him or something. Why so many questions 'bout him? Is there anything I should know?'

'No, no, no. Just wondering.'

'Aha, now I remember, he knew your name…' Before she could finish the sentence Julie interrupted her and saved me.

'So, guys, anyone fancy a banana?'

'Yes,' I said, starving.

'Let's go get one,' she smiled.

It was about half eight and outside it was raining. I was in my room, sitting on my bed trying to do my English homework, when I decided to text Sean. I still had his number in my jacket. I was wondering if he remembered me. It had been only two days since I met him.

But things didn't go as I expected them to. He answered me back saying: 'Hey, would you have Jessica's number by any chance?' This wasn't the answer I was expecting to get. Not at all. I had to read it three times to actually understand what it was saying. What was I supposed to do? Everything was getting so complicated.

I rang Julie. I really needed to hear her voice in that moment.

'Hello,' she answered.

'I need help.'

'Oh, it's good to hear your voice too,' she said.

'Julie, please, this is not the time to mess. Guess what?'

'You're pregnant.'

'No! I'm not, thank God. I am just after finding out Sean likes Jessica.'

'Ha ha... You are joking, right?'

'Does it sound like I am?'

'Well yeah, I think so.'

'No, Julie! It doesn't...'

'OK, OK, I'm sorry, just don't go mad. Why don't you just talk to Jessica and we'll find out what's going on with them. Huh? What do you say?'

'Alright, I guess you're right this time.'

'OK, just promise me you are not going to do anything crazy, just go to bed and not think 'bout this. Promise?'

'OK, I promise.'

'How about I bring you shopping tomorrow?'

'I've no money. The recession is still on in my house,' I said.

'Oh, come on, I can steal my mum's credit card.'

'That's my girl. See you tomorrow. Love you.'

'Love you too.'

Julie always knew what to say and she always found a solution for me.

Next morning I woke up around ten. Julie and I were going to meet at three o'clock at the Spire. It was a sunny day and I really needed to get out of the house for a while.

'What do you think of this dress?'

'I mean, why would she even be interested in him?' I said, talking to myself.

'Right, that's it. I don't know what else to do with you. You're impossible. Not even clothes can distract you.'

'I'm sorry. Am I too obsessed? But, I mean, they only saw each other once right?'

'Ashleigh, you are doing it again.'

'Alright sorry. You were saying about the dress?'

'I was saying it would be nice on you for the next Barcode.'

'Yeah, the colour is really shiny.'

In that moment I turned around with the dress and I saw Jessica. Jessica with Sean.

'That's it, I'm going to kill that bitch!'

I walked out of the shop and that's how the fight started.

I walked out of the shop but the security system started beeping. I realised I was still holding the dress. The security guard came.

'Ma'am, where do you think you are going without paying for the dress?' he asked.

'To fight,' I said handing him back the dress.

I surprised Jessica from the back and started pulling her long black hair.

'Why did you do this to me?' I screamed.

She then started pulling my long blonde hair and she ended up ripping my fake eyelashes off. It hurt like hell.

'I always knew you were wearing fake eyelashes,' she said, trying to be smart.

That's when I heard Julie saying behind me: 'Will you guys stop and sort this out like humans and not animals?'

We both turned around and screamed in her face: 'No!'

The fight was getting more aggressive.

Sean tried to stop us but Jessica and I were so furious that we both ended up punching him on the nose.

That's how Sean ended up in hospital.

After about five minutes an ambulance came and we went to hospital. Blood was all over my T-shirt. I was shaking. What had we done?

'Guys, I'm going to go home,' Julie said. 'I need to babysit my little sister.'

'OK. Don't worry. I'm so sorry for today.'

'Everything will be alright. Let me know how he's doing.'

Then she left.

'How is he doing?' I asked.

'He's much better. He's sleeping now.' Jessica said.

'I'm going to grab a coffee. Can I get you anything?

'No, I'm fine. Thanks.'

While walking on the long corridor, I was thinking about what had happened during that day. I felt bad. Really bad. If I hadn't started that stupid fight, Sean wouldn't have been in the hospital with a broken nose. I was immersed in my thoughts when I bumped into someone.

'I'm really sorry. I was…' That's when I realised that that someone was Keith.

'Ashleigh? What are you doing here?' he said.

'Keith, what a surprise. I didn't expect to see you here.'

'I do voluntary work twice a week here. Is everything alright? You're so pale.'

'It's a long and complicated story…'

'Well, let's go get you some water and you can explain everything to me.'

I explained everything to him and I felt free. For the first time somebody was listening to me and understood me. Then we got interrupted by a nurse.

'Keith, there has been a car accident. I'm going to need you to come with me.'

'I'll be there in a second,' he said to the nurse. Then to me, 'How about we continue our conversation tomorrow night at dinner?'

Dinner? Was I hallucinating?

'So what do you say?' Keith said, a bit worried.

'Yes,' I said smiling at him.

'I'll pick you up at eight.'

A dream coming into reality.

*

Sometimes I wonder is it worth it to fight with a friend over a relationship with Mr Perfect. Two girls fighting over a boy is a desperate attempt by each to save a relationship that was never on. We girls don't realise friends are more important than a boy who is going to hurt us anyway. But if that fight never happened, I would have never discovered the amazing gifts the shy schoolboy had. It's destiny. Some things happen for a reason.

Hope
Dillon Burke

As Randy glanced at the photographs of his beloved mother, he realised how fortunate his life had been before she died. He had always taken things for granted. His mother used to say, 'When life hands you lemons, make lemonade.' He had never understood what she was trying to get across to him and was still trying to grasp it. Randy's life had changed drastically since his mother had died. Randy and his mother were really close, they only had each other. Randy had never met his father.

Ireland in the nineteen sixties was a tough place to live in. Randy Cormack was forced to go to the Kempton Institute as he had no family relatives in Ireland. Now all he had was a cramped room, with dull colours surrounding him. Randy was an only child and always wished he had a brother or sister. Sarah had changed that. Randy met Sarah the first day he arrived at the orphanage. He had been there for the last year and a half, and couldn't take much more. Randy hoped one day him and Sarah would have a house to themselves, where they would enjoy their lives. They had so much in common, and felt good around each other.

Randy was in his room, lying on his bed daydreaming, when Sarah walked in.

'What's up Randy-Dandy?' said Sarah joyfully.

'Oh, hey,' replied Randy. He had not bothered talking to anyone.

'I know you're upset about leaving, and going to a new home, and family but at least one of us is leaving this… DUMP!'

'Yeah, but I don't wanna leave. I wanna stay 'ere with you, you're the only thing I've got left.'

At that moment Sarah just froze on the spot. She finally understood how Randy really felt about leaving the orphanage. She knew he was scared though he had never shown this around her.

'Hey, what about the money we've been saving since you got here. We planned on getting a flat with it… Now it's all going to waste!' said Randy angrily.

They had both earned money by doing chores around the orphanage.

'Oh yeah, forgot about that, huh. Well, maybe we could run away from this joint,' said Sarah sarcastically.

Randy looked right into Sarah's eyes with a weird gaze. He then said: 'That's genius!'

'Hey, I was only kidding,' said Sarah with a little giggle.

Randy's ma had told him if she wasn't around or if anything happened to her to ring her brother. His name was Alan and he lived in England now. He moved there three years ago.

Alan didn't even know his sister had passed away. Randy hadn't really been in contact with him since he had gone to England. Randy wanted to go live with him when his ma died but that hadn't been possible. Randy explained to Sarah that if they got out, they could make it over to England, and live with his uncle until they were old enough to run their own lives. They had enough money to make it to the ferry station but weren't sure how they were going to get there. The ferry station was at the docks which was a few miles away. Randy hadn't been there since he had waved Alan farewell when he left for England. It would be very risky trying to get to England. If they got caught by the police, they would be sent straight to juvenile prison, where the baddest teenagers went when they broke the law.

Randy and Sarah sat down in Randy's room and planned their escape which would take place in three days time. They thought of many ways of escaping but found one that was sneaky and risky, but they believed would work. Three days passed. It was the day of Randy Cormack's leaving but before his departure he had one more chore for Kempton Institute. This was the laundry delivery which involved collecting a big cartload of bed sheets and pillow cases from the laundry room and bringing them outside to the delivery truck. They were then sent to get washed and were returned a week later. Randy was given this chore the day he came to Kempton Institute, and he did it once a week. As he got ready to leave, he started to get changed in his room. He put on his buttoned-up white shirt, tucked it into his greyish brown pants, and then put on his black sports jacket. He parted his light brown hair carefully. He considered how excited he would be when he saw his uncle Alan again and how they would be able to live as a family. As he thought about it, Sarah approached him. He could recognise her a mile away, from the shine of light glittering off her hazel eyes.

'You ready?' said Sarah nervously.

'Yeah, are you?' replied Randy not looking at Sarah and tying his shoe lace.

'Let's hope this works.' He approached the laundry room to collect the laundry cart. He started to wheel it out of the room, when the laundress stopped him.

'I'm gonna miss you m'boy! You keep your head up and don't let anyone put you down. Ya hear me!' said Mary the laundress, with a tear coming down the side of her face.

'Thanks, Mary, I'm gonna miss you too. Don't worry, I will.'

Randy got along very well with Mary. He would always go to her for advice or if he was feeling down. Randy began to bring the laundry out of the entrance's double doors, down the sturdy steep steps and out onto the path, where the truck was waiting. The truck driver beeped his horn twice, and then started to read a newspaper. He was wearing the Eazy-Cleanz grey uniform. Randy was really used to this guy's face as he saw him once a week. As Randy came out the gates of Kempton Institute to load the big white truck, he approached it slowly. He then turned around with the cart and started to run and push it down the big steep road which lay at the corner of Kempton. The guy in the truck started to howl.

'Hey get back here now! Guards, quick! A kid is escaping!' The guards usually didn't really have much to do as the kids in the orphanage were well-raised and well-disciplined. They were well raised but it was still like a prison!

The guards were shocked.

They saw Randy pushing the cart down the hill. At that moment Sarah popped her head out from under the laundry, holding two bags. One contained her own clothes, money and personal belongings, and the other was Randy's.

'We're free!' Sarah cried. Randy felt scared and nervous but also excited and happy. Before he could answer Sarah he saw that they were heading towards a tree. The cart hit the tree and flung them into a bush. In pain, they both rose and started to run off as fast as the wind. Sarah looked back and saw three guards running down the road, but by the looks of it they weren't going to catch up. The guards in Kempton Institute were quite big and extremely lazy.

Randy and Sarah made a run for it into the forest. They changed their clothes, because they knew the police would arrive shortly, searching for them and would recognise them in their other clothing. They ran deeper and deeper into the forest until they found a hollow big enough for the two of them to hide out in.

'You scared?' said Randy nervously.

'No, are you?' said Sarah, almost out of breath.

'No, of course not.'

Trying to sound brave when he really was terrified, Randy didn't want to show his fear. He knew Sarah would then begin to be scared, and that wouldn't get them anywhere. So they lay under the hollow until everything cooled down. As they lay there they dozed off.

Hours later Randy was awoken by the cold air. It had grown darker.

'You OK?' Randy said to Sarah anxiously.

'Yeah, I'm okay, just a bit tired. You know we'll go to juvenile if we get caught?'

'We won't get caught,' said Randy with a commanding voice.

'OK, where to now? How do we get to the dock?'

'I dunno. We'll ask someone after we get out of this forest and get a bite to eat.'

Randy and Sarah continued heading north, until they found a road. As they took to the road, they remained cautious, looking around for anything unusual. They heard a siren going by. They jumped straight back into a bush in the forest. After a few hours of walking through the forest, their hunger started to get to them. They were tired and their mouths were dry. They eventually reached the highway where they saw a sign for the nearest town, Bray. It was two miles away. They decided to start walking before it got too dark. Halfway through their journey to Bray they saw a petrol station which had a shop. They went into the shop but were afraid that the shopkeeper might be aware of their escape from Kempton. Randy opened the door nervously and walked up to the cashier, hoping that he didn't recognise him or Sarah.

'Hello... Em... Can I have two rolls with ham and two lemonades?'

'Okey dokey, I'll make them now.'

Randy placed the money on the counter, looking back out the window to make sure Sarah was OK.

As Randy was about to leave the shop, they heard a radio broadcast, alerting people of an escape from Kempton.

'Two youths from Kempton Institute have escaped and are walking the streets of Dublin, a boy aged sixteen and a girl aged fifteen, please inform us if you have any suspicions.'

The shopkeeper then called Randy back.

'Hey, kid!'

Randy paused for a second, thinking he'd been caught. He turned around slowly.

'Yeah...'

'You forgot your change, kid.'

'Oh, sorry... thank you again,' Randy said, relieved.

Randy and Sarah sat outside on the pavement in no rush to continue their journey. They were exhausted from the long walk.

'Hey, Sarah, look what it says on the side of that truck!'

Sarah looked at the side of a truck parked outside the petrol station, while taking a bite of her roll.

'To Bray and Back...' she read quietly to herself.

They both looked at each other and smiled. Randy knew that Sarah was thinking the same thing he was. As the owner of the truck went into the shop to pay the petrol bill, Randy and Sarah ran over to the truck and jumped in the back. They found a space among the work tools and covered themselves with a big white blanket.

A few minutes later the man came back to the truck and climbed into the driver's seat and set off for Bray. Cold as it was, they tried to have a little nap, but they couldn't. The heavy wind kept lifting the blanket away from them, and they were worried that they would be seen. At last they arrived in Bray. They could smell the salt from the sea water. When the truck stopped at a set of traffic lights the two of them jumped out. They were anxious to get the boat to England.

Randy's head was filled with lots of serious questions. Is Alan still alive? Is he still living in England? Does he have a family now? What if he can't take care of us?

Randy didn't want to think of the negative things. He was a positive guy, but he couldn't get these thoughts out of his mind.

They approached the dock and gazed around, to see if they could see any police. There didn't seem to be any in sight or anyone paying attention to them.

'We did it! We're actually gonna live with someone, and be happy and away from that wretched orphanage,' said Sarah, delighted she'd made it to the dock.

'We haven't done it yet.'

'OK then, let's do it. You ready?'

'Yeah... are you?' Both of them looked at each other and smiled. At this point they could see a glimpse of happiness in the future.

They went up to the desk and asked for two tickets to England.

'OK, can I see your passports please?'

'No problem,' said Randy trying to keep a straight face while smiling.

'There ya go, here's your two tickets. Enjoy your trip.'

They got onto the boat without any hassle. They didn't think it would be that easy. The boat started to take off moments later. They stood in silence and waved back at their old life.

Randy and Sarah looked out from the deck. Their hands rested on the banister of the boat and slowly moved closer and closer to each other. It had been a long night, and finally the sun came up. They gazed at the sky, holding one another's hands.

Junior Night

Graham Burke

My stomach was sick. He gave me the envelope. I wished I was on my own. I could feel my heart thumping. When I got my results I nearly vomited. I didn't look directly at the piece of paper in my hand right away. I covered my eyes and looked at the result of each subject individually. When I was finished, I didn't feel sick anymore; a sudden wave of relief and happiness took over. I started thinking those last three years were worth it. Then I startled myself by screaming 'Yes' at the top of my lungs. But to my shock, nobody was even looking at me. They were too caught up in their own results.

There were three different types of feelings in the room: one was pure happiness, one was sadness and some of the others just didn't care. As soon as I could control my body again I got my twin brother Dillon and my two mates John and Kevin, and we headed for the bus. We were all delighted with our results and enthusiastic about tonight. We got on the bus at Parnell Square and got off at the Cabra Road. I told them, 'I might see you tonight.'

When I got in to my house I put the results on the table and jumped straight into the shower while Dillon went to the baker's with my ma. The shower was lovely and hot. After I washed my hair I got out and went upstairs to get ready. I dried myself off and put on my clothes. I put on my jeans and my G-star jumper and my Addias T-shirt and white Addias runners. Then I started doing my hair. It usually takes me five minutes to do it, but this time it took me fifteen minutes as I wanted to look extra good for tonight. I went downstairs to my ma to show her my results. She had just got back from the bakers with a few little cakes. We sat down at the table. I felt nervous. I was thinking to myself, what if my ma thinks my results aren't that good because my twin got better than me on the Junior Cert?

'I don't think I did that good,' I said to my ma.

'Don't be silly. I don't mind what you got as long as you tried your best,' she replied.

'But Dillon got better than me,' I said.

'It doesn't matter, Graham, you did your best.'

It was just me acting crazy. My ma was over the moon with joy. Then my ma handed me an envelope. I was full of happiness. I tore it open and inside was one hundred euro. I was delighted. I had more than enough for tonight.

'Thanks, ma, you're really good.'

'I'm proud of you, Graham. You did really well. Where are you going tonight?'

'Just going out with my mates.'

'I don't want any messing tonight; there will be a lot of drunken idiots starting fights.'

'I will be alright, ma, there's loads of us.'

'Alright then, enjoy yourself.'

'I will, love you.'

I left the house and headed down to my friend's house. He met me halfway at Phibsboro. His name is Aaron. I've known him since my first day of primary school, he's my best friend. We went down to the Spar to get a roll. When me and Aaron were in the shop, Aaron couldn't control himself as usual and started robbing. He's not that good at robbing so he is always getting us in trouble. The owner of the shop caught Aaron as he was putting his eighth packet of Maltesers in his pocket. He ran at Aaron and grabbed him, shouting at the same time, 'Call the Guards!'

Aaron pushed him against the drinks and all the bottles fell to the ground and smashed. Me and Aaron got out of there as fast as we could. We ran to a nearby lane and laid low for ten minutes. At the end of it Aaron said:

'At least I still have the sweets.'

'Shut up, you nearly got us nicked, ya tick, then we wouldn't be able to go tonight.'

I met up with me other mate. His name is Chad. He is sound. Anyway, I still hadn't got my drink so me and Chad went into the offo. He got me five bottles of Blue Wicked, six cans of Bulmers Pear, and four bottles of Bud. He already had his drink, which Aaron was minding in the playground with Connor and Deco. They are another two of my mates. Me and Chad arrived at the playground with the drink ten minutes later. I went straight up to them.

'Alright? You ready for tonight?' I said.

'Yes, we are,' they replied together.

So we started our cans in the playground and were blaring the music. We were finishing the last can when the Gardaí pulled up outside the playground. I picked up me bottles and jumped onto the wall and carefully jumped down to protect my bottles. My mates did the same thing and we were sprinting up the canal. My mate Mark knew a good spot two minutes away to hide. So we jumped over a back garden and hid in a shed. We were all sweating, we didn't want to get nicked and not be able to go tonight. We sat still and didn't open our mouths for a while when Aaron said,

'They aren't going to find us. Let's finish these bottles.'

So we sat there in the shed and finished our drink. When I had just finished my last bottle, I got a phone call off my mate Matthew from school, but I call him Chucky. He told us him and his mates would meet us at Melodies. Melodies is a Chinese restaurant on Capel Street, and we all get served there. So we all got up and headed to Melodies.

We arrived at seven thirty and we seen Chucky and his mates at the door. So we went into Melodies and ordered our drinks and sat down. While I was talking to Chucky, Aaron got a phone call off Campo; he told Aaron he would be down at eight fifteen with his mate Dugy. We finished off our second pint of Bulmers and headed out the door.

We met Campo at the Centra. We were talking for a while, and then we decided that we needed more drink. So on the way to the bus stop, Chad and Campo went into the offo at Sherrifer. I got another five cans of Bulmers. We walked over to the bus stop across the road.

The bus came within five minutes and we were all buzzing. When we got off we were at the park beside Barcode. I seen three people from me school, Dwayne, Dylan and Graham with two of their mates. I told them I would see them inside Barcode and we walked through the park. It was very dark and there was loads of junkies sitting all over the place doing drugs. They were shouting at us, telling us to f-off. I turned back and saw one of them injecting himself with heroin.

We were halfway through the park when we saw a bench and decided to drink the cans we just got. I was on my second can when these two young ones came over. They were both sixteen. They told us the Garda just took their drink off them. We would hate that to happen to us, so we gave them a can each. I started talking to the small one. Her name was Claire and she was a cracker. She asked me was I with anyone. Then I asked her was she with someone and she said no too. Then we just started meeting. We were meeting for a few minutes when two undercover Garda started walking towards us. We picked up our drink and started running. One of the Garda was really fast and was catching up on me, so I dropped my can and kept running. We hid in a load of bushes and within ten seconds they sprinted by us.

Campo said he was going because he didn't wanna get nicked. We told him we'd talk to him later. So we headed over to get chewing gums in the shop because they don't let you in Barcode if you smell like drink. When we got outside Barcode the line was huge. I looked in my pocket for my ticket and I was shocked to discover it was not there. Now I would have to line up in that queue for ages. After about thirty minutes we finally got in to the club. It was completely full of people. It was so warm in there. People were sneaking in naggins of vodka. There was loads of security standing on chairs all over the place.

We handed our jackets in to the people working there. Then we walked into the place. I already saw loads of people from school. There was loads of good music playing, like Sexy Chick, Boom Boom Pow, Right Round and more good songs. We went into the bathroom and the smell was horrible, somebody had just gotten sick. We decided to get out of there, the smell was getting worse. As we were coming out of the bathroom, Aaron's ex-bird Emily came over and saw Aaron meeting some girl. She went ballistic and started shouting at him. While that was happening the girl quietly snuck off. The two of them sat down at the sofas and Aaron calmed Emily down. He came over to us later that night in Barcode and told us he had got back with her. He was delighted. He had broken up with her over a stupid fight and was happy to be back with her.

Then we heard everyone cheering and turned round to see two fellas swinging hooks at each other. One was a big fat fella and the other was a really skinny tall guy. We all thought the fat fella was going to win, but the skinny guy just dodged all of the other guy's digs and caught him with a knee to the face. At that point the security grabbed both of them and escorted them outside to the Gardaí, who were waiting outside. It all went back to normal five minutes later and me, Chad and the rest of us headed to the dance floor. We were dancing for like five minutes when some girl bumped into me. I turned around and she was a cracker, so I said,

'You with someone?'

'No,' she replied.

At that moment I leaned over and we started meeting. It was near the end of the night and the drink was fully kicked in, I was locked. I met about twenty girls but couldn't remember what their

The Worst Shock Of My Life

John Cooney

She told me to sit down. She said she had something to tell me. The minute she said that, I was worried. I thought she was going to tell me that she had done the dirt on me.

She told me to sit down again.

She was silent for five minutes. It felt like one hour had gone by. Then she started to cry.

I said, 'What's wrong?'

Then she said, 'I'm pregnant.'

I said, 'What? You couldn't be!' It had been only the first time we had done it. 'Are you sure it's my baby?'

She looked at me in horror and said, 'Are you serious? You're the only one I've slept with.'

I stepped up and I put my arms around her. I said, 'Sorry. I'm just in shock. Don't worry, everything is going to be alright. We're going to stick by each other.'

A week went by. I could not sleep for the whole week. I was worried sick. I was worried about what my da or ma were going to say or do. I had many thoughts rushing though my head. Would they tell her to have an abortion or would they kick me out of the house?

Me and Cheryl talked. I told her that the best thing to do was to tell both sets of parents about the shocking news. We decided to tell them both the following Saturday.

The next few days were a nightmare. I couldn't sleep and I couldn't eat. I was in a bad mood for the whole few days.

Finally, that Saturday came. I had a mixture of feelings. I was worried about what to say to my parents.

It was dinner time. We were all sitting around the table. Ma and Da were happy. My ma had got three numbers up in the lotto and she'd won seven hundred euros. She was delighted. I said to myself, 'This is the chance to break the news.'

I said to them, 'I have something to tell yous. Cheryl's pregnant. I'm going to be a da.'

The whole place went quiet.

My da said, 'What? You're going to be a da?'

I anxiously said, 'Yeah.'

Silence fell upon the room. Once again, my parents would not say anything.

I went up to my room and phoned Cheryl, and told her what I had done. I asked her, 'Did you tell your parents yet?', and she said she hadn't had the chance to speak to them. I suggested, 'Would you like the two of us to tell them together?' She jumped on the opportunity and said, 'Yeah.'

I was sitting on my own, worrying sick for about an hour. I heard my parents coming up the stairs. I got more anxious about what they were going to say to me.

I heard my ma call out, 'James, can we come in?'

My heart was thumping.

I answered, 'OK.'

'We're sorry to hear the news about Cheryl. Me and your da have talked it out and we've decided we will support yous when the baby's born.'

Then my da said, 'Do Cheryl's parents know yet?'

I said, 'No. We're going to tell them tonight at seven o'clock.'

My da replied in an anxious tone, 'Good. They need to know about the news.'

My ma came over to me and she give me a hug that felt awkward. But I was relieved.

I called around to Cheryl's house about half six. She met me at her door, then we went in. Cheryl called out to her ma and da, 'Come in. We have something to tell yous.'

'What's wrong? I'll be in in a minute,' said her ma.

With that, Cheryl's da walked in. Then the ma came in.

'What's wrong?' said the ma.

'What is it, Cheryl?' said the da, sharply.

Cheryl said, 'I'm pregnant.'

Cheryl's ma's face went white with the shock. Then the whole room went silent for about five to seven minutes. You could hear all the little kids playing outside, it was so quiet.

Then her ma said, 'I was only saying to your da last night that I've been worried about you, but I was afraid to say anything.'

Her da replied by saying, 'When is the baby due?'

We both said together, 'Around Christmas time.'

Cheryl's ma, Bernie, asked, 'Are yous OK?'

'Yeah, thanks, Ma. I thought you and da were going to kill me. I've been worried what to do. I said at first to James, I'll have to have an abortion because we are so young and we're still in school. But we decided not to have an abortion and to keep the baby. I'm glad we've told you now. James told his ma and da earlier. Maybe James's parents can come around and have some dinner.'

Bernie left the room and went into the kitchen where Cheryl's da was having a cup of tea. He was still getting over the shock.

'Your ma was nicer than I thought she'd be, after all the drama that went on,' I said. 'It's such a relief that we've told both of the parents now. I'll ask my parents to come around to have dinner with your parents.'

Cheryl and I sat down on the chairs. I said, 'When you think of it, like, you have your Leaving Cert in the summer, then a few months later you'll have the baby.'

Cheryl expressed her concerns to me. 'I wonder what is going to happen when I have the baby. What about college? I wonder will my ma help me out with the baby if I go to college. There are so many things going though my head, I don't know what to do.'

I went over to comfort Cheryl and said, 'You should come over to my house and stay the night, after all that's happened. We'll get a good movie and I'll get popcorn as well.'

It was now Friday night. Cheryl had arranged for her parents to meet my parents at my house.

I met Cheryl and her parents at her house and we decided to walk back around to my house where my ma had some dinner cooked for all of us. She wanted to get to know Cheryl's parents better since Cheryl was having her son's baby. She had cooked chicken, potatoes, peas, gravy and carrots. She had wine for the adults and water for me and Cheryl.

I was a bit nervous because it was the first time both parents were going to be meeting each other. I was worried what was going to happen. Were Cheryl's parents going to like mine?

So we left Cheryl's house, and when we were going around to my house Cheryl's ma said to me. 'Has your ma got the food cooked yet?'

When I rang the doorbell my heart was going like ninety.

My ma opened the door.

'Come on in, it's great yous could come around.'

I was starting to feel a bit better already.

Cheryl's ma said. 'What is the beautiful smell? How long will the food be in?'

'I hope yous are hungry. I cooked a lovely meal.'

We'd been talking about how the last few months had flown by. I was saying to Cheryl she had been getting a bit big and she could have the baby a month early.

Cheryl said to me, 'Feel my stomach. I felt the baby kicking.'

Cheryl was happy.

We were all finished the dinner. Cheryl left the dinner table. She was going up to the bathroom.

After a few minutes, Cheryl called me. I ran up the stairs. I said, 'What's wrong?'

I could hear the panic in her voice when she said, 'My water broke.'

With that, I shouted down to my ma, 'Ring an ambulance!'

I began to panic. She was only eight months pregnant.

The ambulance came ten minutes later. It felt like hours had passed by. The ambulance man put Cheryl into the back of the ambulance. Cheryl's ma and my ma went with her.

I was nervous in the waiting room, walking up and down, thinking was she going to have a baby girl or a boy. And wondering was the baby going to be alright. She was only gone eight months. Would the baby be grand or would it be sick?

Two hours later my ma came out to me and said, 'She had a baby girl and everything's going to be OK.'

I was so happy and relieved that she'd had the baby and it was OK. I couldn't wait to see the baby. After half an hour, I went down to see her. First, they'd needed to clean the baby, and Cheryl had to recover.

I left Cheryl in the hospital and went home. There was nobody there. I looked back at the past eight months. At the start, it was the worst shock of my life but it turned out to be the happiest moment of my life.

The Creak

Kevin Cooney

I couldn't get to sleep the night before the Junior Cert results. I was awake till all hours wondering what I had got. I was up really early for school. For the first time ever I was there before the bell went. We all sat in the class talking.

'Did you sleep last night?' I whispered to Carlos.

'No, I couldn't stop thinking about the results.'

'Neither could I. I just couldn't get to sleep.'

Everyone was anxious. You could feel the tension in the room. As it got closer to the results being given out I was less nervous. We knew it would be at about 10.30.

At 10.20, Mr Healy's voice came over the intercom.

'Would all last year's third year's come to the atrium now, please?'

I started to feel nervous all over again. I was finally getting my Junior Cert results.

I was waiting for my name to be called out. It seemed to take forever. I was really scared when I got the envelope. My heart was thumping. I opened it slowly. I got six honours and one fail. I was so happy.

'What did you get?' I asked David and Carlos.

I don't remember what they said, but I know they were happy. There was a lot of excitement in the atrium.

'Are you still going to Bondi?' I asked Seán and Adam.

'Yeah, can't wait, it should be a good laugh.'

'I'll ring you later to arrange a time to meet up.'

Me, Richie, Seán and Adam were all going out to celebrate together.

'Where's Bondi anyway?' asked Richie.

We all laughed because he had his ticket. He was always in a world of his own.

'It's on the quays, you twat.'

'Will we go to KFC first so we can go out early?'

'Great idea,' said Richie. 'Talk to you later.'

We met up at half five. I thought they would never finish their bottles. They were taking forever to drink them.

'Come on lads, I wanna get something to eat before we go to Bondi. I'm starvin!'

I finally dragged them to KFC. Then we went to Bondi.

'Oh shit, look at the queue. It'll take ages to get in,' said Seán.

'You're lucky you're with me,' I said. My uncle works on the door so we don't have to line up.'

'I knew you'd come in handy sometime,' slagged Seán.

It was so packed when we got in we had to squeeze by people.

'Jesus, it smells bad in here,' I said to Adam.

'Yeah I know. I don't think I can stick it.'

As I was pushed by a table I heard someone say, 'This is muck.'

They were right!

'We'll give it an hour,' said Adam. 'If it doesn't get any better by then we'll leave.'

'Yeah, OK.'

It got better! More people got up to dance. The music was good. They even played Akon.

'Do you still wanna go home?' I asked Adam.

'No, it's getting good!'

Me, Seán and Adam got talking to three girls.

'What age are you?' I asked the one with the blonde hair.

'Sixteen. What about you? Where are you from?'

'Town.'

'You're not giving too much away, are you?' she said. 'Me and some of my friends are going to a house party later on. Do you wanna come?'

'Yeah, OK where's it on?'

'Meath Street. It's not too far from here. By the way my name is Tammy!'

'Oh yeah, I forgot to ask! I'm Paul. Can Seán and Adam come too?'

'Yeah, if they want to.'

I pushed my way through to ask them.

'Tammy wondered if we wanna go to a party, what do you think?'

'Yeah, sounds good. Where's it on?'

'Meath Street.'

'How are we going to get there?' asked Seán.

'We'll all bunch in and get a taxi over.'

I made my way back across the dance floor to Tammy.

'Yeah, we're all going to go. We'll meet you outside to get a taxi.'

I could see she was pleased. That felt good. Maybe I was going to get lucky.

Finally we hopped into a cab. At last we were on our way to the party. We were feeling very giddy. The drink had gone to our heads.

'We're going to get lucky tonight,' I whispered to Adam.

'Shut up,' Adam said. 'They'll hear you.'

Tammy had heard me. She hit me a slap but I knew she was messing. I was hoping it meant she liked me.

The taxi pulled up outside a house. The music was really loud.

'This is obviously it!' I said to Seán.

There were cans and bottles in the garden. There were people everywere. I knew a few faces. Some of them didn't look in the best of form, they were a bit all over the place. There was a lot more people inside.

'Where can we get a drink?' I asked a lanky fella standing near the door. At that stage I needed a drink.

'There is some on the kitchen table.'

'Do you want to come with me to get a drink?' I asked Tammy.

'Yeah, OK.'

We got a drink and went out the back to sit on a wall. She was good to talk to and a really good listener. We sat on the wall for a long time.

'Adam seems to be gone missing with your mate,' I said to Tammy.

'Yeah, she liked him,' said Tammy.

'Do you do any sport or dancing?' I asked.

'Yeah I do a bit of dancing at the weekend.'

'Are you any good? Will I see you on "Ireland's Got Talent" any time soon?'

'I wouldn't have the bottle to do it on my own, maybe sometime if I could form a group.'

'If you ever go on it, you're guaranteed a vote from me!'

'At least I know I'll get one vote then! What do you do when you're not at parties?'

'I keep myself occupied.'

'Are you trying to be mysterious?' she laughed.

'Ah no, I'm only messing. I play football.'

'Are you any good? Who do you play for?'

'Have you not heard of me? I play for Bohs.'

'I don't really watch football.'

We chatted some more and then went back inside. I was feeling knackered at this stage. It had been a long day. We squashed into a corner of the couch.

'Are you tired?' Tammy asked.

'Yeah, a bit, but it's more that I'm getting fed up here.'

'Thanks a lot,' said Tammy.

'Ah no, not with you.'

'Do you want to come back to mine? My mum and dad are away for the night.'

'That sounds good. I could even stay!'

'Yeah, sure,' she laughed. 'Well… actually… my mum and dad would never know if you stayed. But what about your mum?'

'Easy, I'll text her and tell her I'm staying in Seán's.'

'OK.'

'Get ready for the best part of the night,' I said to Tammy.

'You should be so lucky,' she laughed.

I really liked her but was feeling a bit guilty.

We walked to her house because it wasn't that far from the party. As we were walking back, we were talking about how good the night was.

'I can't believe I didn't ask you what you got in your Junior?' said Tammy.

'I got nine honours and one fail.'

'You did better then me anyway,' she said.

When we got to the house Tammy said, 'Be quiet, my sister's asleep upstairs.'

'OK.'

I sat in the sitting room while Tammy went upstairs for a minute. I was looking around at all the family photographs; there was some amount of them! I was starting to feel guilty again, and a bit nervous. She came back down and said her sister wasn't there.

'Are you going to look for her?' I asked.

'No, she's a big girl now and we don't want to be disturbed.'

'What do you mean?'

'I'll be back in a minute,' she laughed.

A few minutes later she came through the door struggling with two pillows and a duvet. We finally got comfortable on the sofa. We must have fallen asleep.

'Quick, quick, wake up Paul, I hear a key in the door.'

I jumped up. My heart was going ninety.

'Will I hide?' I asked Tammy.

'There's no time, just act normal.'

A man and a woman walked in. I knew it had to be her ma

and da. I felt weak because I didn't know what they were going to say.

'Who is this, Tammy?' asked her da.

'This is Paul. He needed somewhere to stay so I let him stay on the sofa.'

'Paul, I think it's time for you to go. We need to talk to Tammy,' said her da.

I couldn't get out of the house quick enough.

Now I was worrying about my ma. I was wondering if she had found out about me not being in Seán's house. I was also thinking about Tammy and if she would get in much trouble. As I turned the corner I saw my house and was happy to see there were no lights on. When I got to the front door I remembered I had to be quiet going upstairs because the third step had a creak in it. As I climbed over the third and onto the fourth I remembered it was the fourth that made the creak! I stood still for a moment but nobody woke up. All I could hear was my heart thumping. I could only relax when I closed the door of my own room. I was still worried my ma would come in and ask questions. But she didn't. I couldn't go to sleep. I had so many thoughts in my head. I was hoping Tammy's ma and da weren't giving her too much of a hard time. I kept checking my phone to see if I had got any messages from her.

I must have fallen asleep because the next thing I knew the light was coming in the window. I checked my phone when I woke up and there was a text! I texted her back immediately.

'Did your ma and da freak?'

'They weren't too impressed but they were OK about it. Did you get home alright? It was a good night wasn't it?'

'Yeah, it was alright. I'm glad you weren't in too much trouble I got home fine, no one woke up. I'm still a bit wrecked though. Ttyl.'

I was thinking about Tammy all day so in the end I rang her.

'Hello Tammy... how are you getting on?'

'Grand... nice to hear your voice again.'

My heart was thumping. I really did like her. What was I going to do?

'Do you wanna go to the pictures later?' she asked.

'Ehm… I'll have to get back to you on that one. I was meant to be meeting my girlfriend tonight.'

Hangman
Robert Courtney

I started my career in a little club in Dublin called Crumlin United. My club was quite good. They had good facilities, such as an astro pitch and other pitches.

One day I had a match. It was the semi-final of the Cup. There was a scout at the match, so everybody was trying to impress. But I didn't, because I was just trying to play my normal game. The match was fast, quick football. Tackles were flying in, basically end to end football. I scored two goals. I was delighted.

The scout came over to me at the end of the match and asked me if I would come over for a trial at Manchester United. I was delighted with the opportunity to get a trial with a big club like that. It was always a dream to play for the team I had supported as a boy.

The day came. It was all exciting because it was a once in a lifetime opportunity. It was make or break for me. I had only one fear, travelling on airplanes—it wasn't my thing. My mam and dad dropped me at the airport. I was boarding my plane and I was still nervous. I was on the plane now and there was a man with a hat on him. It was Wayne Rooney. I was shocked. I was all shy, talking to him. He said, 'Are you going over to Manchester for a trial?'

I said, 'Yeah.'

Wayne told me, 'Good luck.'

I arrived in Manchester. It was very cold. The manager had

picked me up at the airport and he asked me if I was excited. I said, 'Yeah, very excited and nervous.'

We arrived at the training ground. It was class. I met the players that I would be training with. They were all sound. I had my first training session with the team. It was class. The manager liked the style of football I played.

The week was coming to an end. Today was my last training session with the team. I was ready to go and all the boys asked the manager to sign me, they said I was a good player. So the manager said, 'I'll think about it.' I was delighted.

I went home and I was back playing with my normal team. It felt weird because the standard of the Manchester United players was so much better. I had the final of the Cup that week. We were playing Cherry Orchard and they were one of the best teams in the league.

The day of the Cup Final was exciting. The match kicked off. There were no real chances in the first half. The second half kicked off. We had chances but we weren't taking them. There were three minutes left. The ball got played in to me. I was one-on-one with the goalkeeper. I shot and I scored. We won the Cup. It was the best thing I ever did.

My dad came over to me at the end of the match and said, 'The manager from Manchester United rang me and told me that he wants to sign you.'

I told all my friends. They were all chuffed for me.

I went over to Manchester and I signed a seven-year contract.

Seven years later...

I was playing in the youth team with Manchester United. It was class, playing against top players week in and week out. I was playing a more central midfield role at Manchester.

The first team had a match against Man City this weekend. It was in the FA Cup. Michael Carrick and Anderson were out injured. Alex Ferguson called me up to the first team. So I got my debut against City. It was amazing.

The match was kicking off. I was nervous. We had no real chances in the first half but we sure did dominate. The second half began and I took a free kick and it went in off the cross bar. The crowd was screaming my name.

I got fouled outside the box. My leg was hurting me, so I got subbed out. I went in to the physio. He did scans on my leg; it was really sore.

I went back to the physio and he said there was bad and bad news only. I had to retire. I was shocked. I was only twenty-two, and I had to retire.

I rang my dad and he said, 'Don't worry. You can play lower league football, son.'

I said, 'Alright, Dad.'

I went home to my wife. She said, 'What's the news?' and I told her that I had to retire from football. She just hugged me and started saying, 'It's alright, babe...'

I just went up to my room and locked myself in it.

I was depressed because I couldn't play football anymore and that was all I ever wanted to do. My wife was calling me and I didn't answer. She was screaming, 'Open the door!' but I just wouldn't answer.

I kicked the stool.

I was found hanged. It was frightening for my family.

Last Gasp Goal

Carlos Donovan

It was a scorcher of a day in the middle of July. Lee's team was playing in the All-Ireland Under-15s Final. They were after beating four great teams along the way and now they were facing a team from Cork. Before he left home to play the match Lee felt really nervous. He kept checking to make sure he had all of his gear in his bag. He couldn't eat his breakfast and he kept moving and kicking his legs. His team was to meet at twelve but Lee was so anxious he arrived at the grounds at half eleven.

Lee was really dedicated to football. It had always been in his dreams to be a footballer. He just loved the game. He put a lot of work into it. He ate properly. He went to bed early. He tried to rest before playing with his team every Sunday. At training every Tuesday and Thursday he always performed very well. Lee lived in a rough part of the city. He was a bold kid when he was growing up but when he got into football he calmed down a lot and football became a major part of his life. To go from living in a rough part of town to making it to the top level in football would be a great achievement for him. Ever since he started playing football, Lee's dad had supported him. He always brought him to training during the week and to his matches at the weekend. If he needed new boots his dad would buy them for him. Lee had blue eyes and long black hair—the same as his father. His father was Spanish. He had come to Dublin when he was twenty years old and had got a job in a bank. He worked his way up and was now a branch manager in the Bank of Ireland.

Finally it was time. The match kicked off. Lee still felt nervous. He thought to himself that he would have to work harder. He could see the scout in the corner with his big coat on. The scout was standing there with his notepad. Lee felt a big burst of energy through his body. He was so anxious and determined to impress. He remembered what his coach had said to him that morning, 'Stay relaxed and focus on your own game—ignore the scouts.' Lee's team was playing well but Lee was getting frustrated. He wasn't getting enough of the ball. This frustration carried on as the big defender kept niggling at Lee. He was marking him out of the game so Lee got angry and he snapped. He gave the defender a horrendous foot tackle. The boy was crippled on the ground and was in serious pain. The referee called Lee over to have a word with him.

'Hey, calm down and watch those vicious tackles.'

'Will you snap out of it, Ref, I was going for the ball!'

'Watch your mouth, young man,' replied the referee, producing a yellow card.

Lee wasn't happy to have got a card but in his head he was delighted that the defender had to leave the pitch. Then he was over the moon when he saw the manager's son come on as a replacement. He was a dreadful defender and wouldn't be able to cope with Lee's skills.

After forty minutes Lee still wasn't playing too well. He was letting the scout get to his head. He wanted to impress him so much. There was shouting from the sidelines. He could hear his manager yelling, 'Buck yourself up or you're comin' off!'

Lee's best memory as a young boy was the time he went to an Ireland match. They played Italy in a World Cup qualifier. It was during the summer of 2009. The match had sold out. Lee and his friends had no tickets or any money to buy one so the only way they could think of getting to the match was by bunking in. He was waiting outside nervously thinking about what would happen if he got caught. He saw a little kid walking in with a ticket. A rush of blood shot to his head. He ran over to the barrier. The kid had given in his ticket and he was about to twist the barrier when Lee burst through behind him and ran with excitement. He had made it into the match! Ireland were winning. The whole stadium was buzzing so when it came to the last minute and Italy scored the whole stadium went into shock. Lee and his mates were all emotional and nearly crying. Despite the draw, the Irish players did a lap of honour after the match and applauded the fans. Lee felt it would be a great honour to wear the green jersey one day and feel the support of the crowd.

The second half of the match began. After the manager told Lee to buck up in the first half, he started to play well. He focused more on the game and he was no longer aware of the scout. For the first time in the match Lee got the ball in a great position to score and he fluffed his chance. But this gave him a bit more confidence. It was much later in the match when Lee got his final shot on goal. He received the ball and made a laugh of the hopeless defender by putting the ball through his legs. Then with his clever football brain he chipped the goalkeeper and scored!

'Yeeeeeeessssss!' the sideline shouted.

The manager joined in the celebrations, running down the line, 'Yes, you little beauty ya!'

The other team looked on in disbelief as Lee and his team-mates ran amuck celebrating. Two minutes later the referee blew the whistle. It had ended in a 1-0 victory. Lee's wonderful goal had led them to their first All-Ireland trophy. Lee ran over to his dad after the match. His dad was always honest with him. 'You hadn't the best of games, but boy, you done me proud,' he said and he put his arm around him and gave him a big hug.

The scout came walking towards them after the game. He shook Lee's hand.

'We could do with a few players like you over in Liverpool,' he said. Lee then got a hint that the scout was interested in him. The nerves came back but this time he was excited. The scout told Lee, 'I was watching you the last few games and you have impressed

Stan's The Man

Josh Douglas

It all started when I was in primary school. I was standing in the yard eating my sandwiches when Mick, the school bully, stormed over. I felt completely terrified.

'Give me your sandwich,' he growled and snatched it from my hand. He laughed at my sandwich because my mother cut off the crust.

'Look at these girly jam sandwiches,' Mick laughed.

'Oh my God, who gave you them black eyes, Daniel! Get up to the bathroom now and put on the hot water, I'll follow you up in a minute.' My mother followed me up with a sponge and bathed my eyes.

'Get your coat on, we're going down to the boxing club now.'

'No, I don't want to go down there, Ma. I'm afraid, don't make me. I don't want to fight.'

'You'll be grand and I'll be waiting outside for you.'

The first training session went well, I was fighting people the same age and size as me, so I enjoyed it very much. I didn't want to stop doing it. A few weeks later in the playground, Mick the bully tried to take my money. He grabbed me by the tie and growled at me.

'Give me your money!'

But I gave him the black eyes this time.

*

My first fight. I was never so happy when I heard those words. I was against a boy from the inner city. The training was very intense and very tiring. The sparring was the toughest and all the rest of the training was easy.

My mother woke me up on Monday morning. The nerves were getting to me and I was hoping I was going to win. My opponent was very small but he was strong and very quick. The fight was on the South Circular Road in the National Stadium. I went into the dressing rooms with my trainer, Paddy, and we just went over the stuff we were going to do.

It was my turn to fight and as I was walking out, I saw my opponent. His name was Anto. He had a tattoo of a pair of boxing gloves on his left arm and a big scar under his eye. When the bell rang for the first round of three, I thought it was going to be easy because of his height but it was very tough. He was hitting me so hard and so fast that I couldn't react fast enough. He pushed me up against the ropes and just kept hitting my body. The bell rang for the end of the round. My mouth was bleeding, even through the gumshield. I was very surprised by what this little monster could do. When the bell rang for the second round, I saw my mother in the front row of the audience, cheering for me. During the second round, he was winning again and I was starting to get annoyed. The bell rang and I went to my corner. Paddy was going mad at me, screaming:

'Why aren't you beating this guy? You are much better.'

So the bell rang for the last round and I started to box properly. Anto tried to push me up against the ropes again but I knew what he was doing and I ducked and gave him a powerful right hand on the chin and put him on the ground. The ref started to count and Anto tried to get up on seven but he had no chance. When the ref called ten, I was delighted. I shook hands with Anto and then went down to my ma. The crowd was shouting: 'Stano, Stano.'

I couldn't believe it. When I went to school the next day, Mick the bully laughed at me because of my black eye from the night before.

I said: 'What are you laughing at?'

He ran at me with his hand raised, but when I raised mine he flinched and ran the opposite way. I won every fight up until I was eighteen, including fighting Anto again in a tournament.

Four years later, I was in my house. It was the morning of a big amateur fight. I saw a flashy BMW pull up outside my house but I didn't recognise the car. A man in a nice suit got out and knocked on my door. My mother answered and I heard them talking for a minute, then he came into the kitchen where I was eating my breakfast. He said:

'Daniel, I'm offering you a promotion. Will you accept to go pro?'

'Of course I will, when do I start?'

'Tonight. I have a fight for you against a man from England. His name's David Galvin.'

I was so excited about getting the promotion, so I decided to go out on the beer that night. Me and my two friends, Dylan and Jake, went to a pub in town and towards the end of the night we got into a bit of trouble. When we were walking to get a taxi, two men our age started raising trouble but we just kept walking. The two of them jumped on Dylan, so me and Jake jumped in. I was going crazy and I just kept hitting the man, even when he was on the ground. A taxi man broke up the fight and the police were called. Because I went so crazy and left him in such a bad state, I got arrested and charged. Two weeks later, I was up in court and the judge told me I was getting locked up for three weeks. I said to myself: 'My boxing career is over.'

When I went home, my mother and promoter were in my house and they looked disgusted. After I told them about the jail sentence, my promoter didn't want anything to do with me. I felt so bad and I knew I had just let my mother down. When I went to jail, it was so boring sitting in a cell for twenty hours a day but I trained every chance I could. When I came out, I couldn't even go back to my old club or to Paddy. Word had spread and no club would take me. I went home, apologised to my mother and told her that no club would take me. I said to her: 'I won't make you proud now.'

And she said: 'You have already made me proud.'

I was sitting in my house one day and my friend Dylan knocked on my door screaming:

'You have a fight against Jonny Moore from America.'

It was for charity and I was so happy. I trained myself for two months, went to the gym every day and put myself through hell. I could not believe how fit and strong I got in those two months.

The night before the fight, I was lying in bed and I started getting nervous because I hadn't been in the ring for so long. The morning of the fight, I had my breakfast and then took it easy, while going over my tactics in my head. I got a knock on my door, it was Jonny Moore. He was much bigger in person. He said to me:

'Daniel. This is just for charity, so let's just take it easy, OK?'

I replied and said: 'OK. I'll see you tonight.'

And shook his hand.

So, later that night, Jake gave me and Dylan a lift to the club for the fight. When I got there, I went into the dressing room for a half hour and I went over my tactics and just relaxed. It was time for the fight when the commentators called us out. We both got into the ring while the commentators were talking about the charity and how much money it had raised. We raised €4,500 at €30 a ticket. The bell rang, we shook hands and who knows what happened.

Addiction
Ashleigh Eyre

A woman I know a long time now once had a very bad drug addiction. By the time she was twenty-one, she had three children and had absolutely no time at all for them. This all started off with her at a young age, she had a lot of troubles as a little girl and I guess it just followed on from there. Shelly got expelled from school at the age of fourteen as she never came in and when she bothered coming to school she never did any work, had no homework done, never wore full uniform and tried to bring other students down with her. This told the teachers she didn't want to be in.

Shelly was also a very talented girl. When she was in 5th class, she entered the school play and was given the main role for her amazing voice. It is a pity she took the wrong road.

By the time she was seventeen she was expecting a baby. Shelly had no money, no job, not a lot of education and also herself and her boyfriend had only split up. Some students and past teachers described her as disruptive, ignorant, boring and very aggressive. Stories had been sent around saying she was taking all kinds of drugs and constantly drinking. She was also a big bully and did not have any friends because she wouldn't communicate with anyone. Shelly lived with her parents until she was eight years old. Her mother and father didn't have the best life when they were young either, but it was a lot different back then than it is now. They grew up in the inner city and they just got in with the wrong group of people and went downhill from there.

One day Shelly rang her mother to go for coffee and discuss matters face to face. They finally met up and Shelly went up to the counter. She ordered two cappucinos and some chocolate biscuits for herself and her mother. Shelly's mother offered to pay for them but Shelly replied instantly, 'No, Mam, I have money here.' They finally sat down and started drinking their coffee and began to chat. Shelly began to cry and her mother asked, 'Shelly, darling, what's wrong?'

Shelly said back, while stirring her coffee and drying her eyes: 'I'm going the wrong way, Mum. I can't waste my life like this anymore.'

Shelly's mother waited for a few seconds to answer. She then said: 'This is why I agreed to come for a coffee, to have a chat about you and your life. You're going down the wrong track in life totally, love.'

Shelly looked at her mum and instantly turned away.

'Why does it have to be me, Mum?'

Shelly's mother replied with a whisper, as she had food in her mouth.

'Well, honey, it was your choice of life, you made the decisions, now you have to deal with them. Only you can change it.'

Shelly asked her mum did she want another coffee but her mum insisted she would get this one. While they continued their conversation, Shelly said to her mum, 'I'm going to get help.' She had copped on and had realised she had children to look after. Shelly's mother was delighted to hear her daughter say that. Shelly was such a beautiful girl and it was a very bad description of her that was given by past pupils. As Shelly told her mum, she was going to change and we all hoped she'd just stick to her word.

Shelly found a lovely apartment with two bedrooms—just enough for her two boys in one room and herself and the new baby in the other. Her kids were gorgeous but, as I heard, they had no manners at all—well, would you expect anything different? Shelly was trying her best to get on track but as most of her life had been taken over by drugs, it was hard!

Shelly went forward to sign up for her apartment and they gave her a date for an interview. She attended the interview and everything went well, as she hoped. The interviewer commented, saying that she wasn't very well dressed and she looked like a messy woman. He also said that her kids looked like animals and that he would have to check back on the previous apartments and flats she had lived in.

A few weeks later, the interviewer texted Shelly.

He said: 'Hey Shelly, I've looked back on your previous flat in ballymun.'

Shelly replied: 'OK thats fine so do I get the apartment?'

Shelly got nervous as it took him a good ten minutes to text back.

Shelly finally got a reply.

'Well Shelly it's not that easy as I have checked and found out that you missed a few payments of rent and didn't really keep your apartment clean.'

Shelly got very angry and gave him a smart message back.

'Well as you should know I do have three children and I try to clean as much as I can.'

The interviewer wrote back: 'I know yes, but the thing is, I have this apartment fully furnished and newly done up and I don't really want to let someone go live in it who is going to let their kids scribble all over my walls and wreck the furniture. As long as you have some discipline over them, I guess you're in.'

Shelly screamed with delight.

'THANK YOU very much and don't worry bout that, everything will be in place.'

She sent him another message, saying: 'When do I collect the keys and where?'

He replied back: 'I'll ring you at 12 o'clock tomorrow and give you the address.'

'OK tata fine cya then,' Shelly wrote back.

That night Shelly and her family were very excited, they were packing bags and getting everything ready. Soon Shelly received a message.

'I've just been in a meeting with your ex landlord. He told me a lot of things I hadn't been told bout your parties all night, drunken fights. I also heard a lot of guards have been involved. I can't have this, I'm not giving you this apartment. I'm sorry.'

Shelly didn't answer the text because she was in shock. She was devastated and angry, as he had no reason to check up with anything from the past. Shelly was really looking forward to moving on and trying to get her life back on track.

Four months later.

Shelly has not tried to move on at all. She has been living the same way since she had her children. I would really like her to change but I don't think now is the time. She should get her life on track. Get away from everyone and just sort out her problems.

She could do with a break.

Chase The Cake

Rebecca Heary

'Your turn,' said the well-built man in his clean-cut uniform.

I stood up and followed him into a big room, which was dark but had a bright light in the middle of it. The light shone on a desk with a few pieces of paper on it. I sat on the nearest chair to me. As I looked around, another man walked in. He looked so business-like as he sat on the other side of the desk. He didn't say anything for a while; just sat there staring at me with a knowing look in his eyes. I was a little panicky but tried to stay calm. He took a deep breath and then said, 'Right.'

I looked over at my cousin Jessica, guessing she was as nervous as me.

'You know why you are here, right?' he asked, a sneaky smile coming through in the corner of his mouth.

I nodded, playing with the zip on my jacket.

'What did you think you were doing? Thought yous were funny? Mad? Or were ya just not thinking?'

I hesitated.

'Ehh... well, I don't really know,' I said.

I glimpsed Jessica from the corner of my eye. She didn't answer at first, just kept her head down. I knew she didn't want to talk but I wasn't going to take all of it.

'So? What was in your mind then, miss?' he said impatiently to Jessica.

'What she said,' Jessica replied, panicky.

I don't think he believed us, though, because he just let out a big sarcastic laugh.

Then he jumped up. Told us that he'd be right back. As soon as he left the room, Jessica turned and looked at me, angrily.

'What?' I said.

'You knew I didn't want to talk,' she said.

'I know, but neither did I,' I said. 'Think of what my mam will say? I won't be allowed go away now.'

'Don't be stupid, Becky,' Jessica replied. 'You're obviously going to be going away. They already booked and paid for it, so they can't just not bring you.'

'Yeah, I suppose,' I said. 'What do you think your dad's going to say?'

'I don't know,' said Jessica. 'Don't really wanna know either; like I'm shitting it.'

'Ya know what?' I sat up in the chair. 'I say we should have a little Charlie's Angels moment and make a run for it.'

Jessica looked at me as if I were completely mad.

'Are you for real?' she asked.

'Yeah, like seriously,' I said. 'No one's here and we know how we got here, so we know how to get out.'

I jumped up, ran to the door and opened it slightly. I stuck my head out, looked left then right. I pulled my head in and shut the door fast but quietly. Jessica sat there shocked, her mouth wide open. I don't think she thought I was for real.

'I don't think this is a good idea,' she said.

She looked at the papers on the table, then snatched a sheet. I didn't know why, but I was too excited to care. Getting ready for our little mission. We went to open the door, but as I reached for the handle it moved. We hid behind the door. It opened. Someone took a step in. We took a deep breath and held it in. From behind the door I could see the head of the freaky business man. He was in shock, staring at an empty room. He slammed the door, leaving us in the room again. We exhaled with relief.

'Right, let's go,' Jessica said nervously.

'No, not yet,' I said. 'It won't be clear. Let's just catch our breath then we'll go,' I told her, leaning against the wall.

I opened the door slowly. I looked around for the bad guys in the black suits. We crept down the dark narrow hall, pressed close against the wall. We saw a room up ahead. As the room got nearer, we heard it. The voice. The man who had caught us the first time. He was looking for us; getting his minions to help. I grabbed Jessica and pulled her into a different room and shut the door behind us.

'What?' Jessica whispered.

'The big fella is looking for us. He's in that room across from us.'

Jessica opened the door slightly and looked out.

'What do you see?' I asked.

'Shh!' she said, listening to the big fella in the other room. 'Do you know were Door B is?' she shut the door.

'What? Why?' I asked.

'He's putting his guards at that door to stop us,' she said.

'That's the main door,' I said. 'I know another one.'

I peeked outside. The coast was clear.

'Come on,' Jessica whispered loudly.

We ran over to the far wall and pressed up against it, going step by step, very slowly. No one was left in the room next door. Guess they all went to Door B to stop us. Ran again. Turned the corner sharply to see a group of them waiting. Turning back around the corner. Ran, pulling Jessica with me.

'Where now?' said Jessica.

I looked around. 'This way,' I said, running to the main part of the building. 'Hide,' I said, 'hide because they're right behind us.' I ran and hid behind a rack. Jessica came to hide beside me. I glared at her.

'When I told you to hide I didn't mean come with me! Split up!' I said, holding my hands out in frustration.

'Oh! Sorry,' Jessica said with a little giggle.

She was about to go but I pulled her back.

'Ouch! What now?' Jessica said, holding her neck.

I pointed over to the way we came from.

'There's the fellas. Look,' I said.

Two men and a giant stood on a platform, all in black. They stood aside to let the main man through. The one with the voice. He looked around, so serious. Then they split up to find us. I crept along, behind the rack and looked to see were they went. They were gone. I waved for Jessica to follow. We started to run again.

'Over there,' I pointed to another door.

But when we turned there was a big, huge giant in black. We ran fast. Faster. Jessica beside me. Ran through people and racks of things. The giant chased us, knocking things down. We tried to put stuff in his way.

'Jessica! Full speed!' I said.

She nodded and started to laugh. On we ran. At the corner of my eye I saw the main fella again. I stopped with a smile and waved at him. He still looked serious but I know there was a smile coming out. I ran back to Jessica's side and as soon as we got to the door we slowed down. Caught our breath, knowing we'd got away safe and sound. We jogged up the road but I kept looking back thinking someone was coming behind us. When we got near the bus stop we looked at each other and started laughing.

'Ahh... here... what do we get ourselves into, ha!' I said.

'Yeah I know. I blame you...' Jessica said, laughing.

We got to the bus stop right on time for the bus.

'And it's a Number 40 and all. Come on,' Jessica said as I was reaching in my pocket for the money I had.

I paid myself on and went upstairs and right behind me was Jessica.

'What time is it?' I asked

'Eh... it's going on half seven,' she said.

'And we went in at two. Do ya think our mams will say something?'

'No! We're usually back at eight anyway.'

'Yeah, I suppose. Ah that was good; my master plan worked,' I said giggling while we relaxed at the back of the bus.

'Yeah, but it was your master plan that got us there in the first place,' she said with an attitude that was, well, calling me stupid.

'No, you're the one that was too slow and loud,' I said.

'Here, don't be putting the blame on me!' she shouted at me.

I looked over to her crossing my arms.

'Alright. Sorry.'

We were nearly home. Jessica asked if I was going to her house.

'No, I'm going to go home and get me dinner. I'm starving.'

'Yeah, same here. Where's your phone?' she said curiously.

'Here,' I took me phone out from me pocket. 'Why?' I said.

'I can't find mine,' she said.

'Check your bra,' I said, because that was usually where I put all my stuff.

'Eh, Becky, it's a phone. Sure there wouldn't be any room down there with these puppies,' she said messing with her bra.

'Ha ha, then they must be little Chihuahua puppies cause they're tiny,' I said, still laughing.

'Shut up, you! Just because your boobs aren't a normal size.'

'It's not my fault and here, your stop's next.'

'Alright, yeah, thanks. I'll talk to ya later,' she said, walking to get off. 'Oh! And what a team we make,' she shouted.

I started to laugh. How on earth did that all work? How did they not catch sixteen-year-old girls? I got off at my stop and started to walk to my house, looking around every road I walked past to see if I could see anyone I knew and so on, but no one was out, not even a dog. Outside my house I stood there for a moment trying to think of anything to say as to why I was late but nope, I got nothing.

Knock, knock. I waited at the door to be let in.

'Heya,' I said to my ma.

'Heya. Eh, home late?' my ma said, following me into the kitchen, waiting for an answer.

'Eh, well, I was having fun,' I said. 'Me and Jessica just walked around, found a few mates and forgot about the time,' I lied. 'Sorry,' I said, looking at the ground and trying to keep a straight face.

'Oh, OK. Your dinner is over there when you want it,' said me mam.

'Thanks, I'm just going upstairs for a bit,' I replied.

I ran upstairs and tried to ring Jessica but no answer. Then I remembered that she lost her phone so I rang her house phone.

'Hello, is Jessica there?' I said.

'Yeah, just a minute. I'll get her now,' said her mam.

'Hello?' Jessica picked up the phone.

'Heya, it's Becky. Did your mam say anything?'

'Nope. Just about my phone, but it's all good. You?'

'Nope. Looks like we got away with it,' I said with a big smile on my face.

'I'm having a game of Fifa,' said Jessica. 'I'll ring ya tomorrow, OK?'

'Alright, I'll talk to ya later,' I replied.

I lay on my bed for a while and felt really tired. So I got changed and went to bed and then blacked out.

A beam of sunlight woke me up. I turned around trying to go back to sleep but I couldn't. I sat up and looked around. It was half ten. I did the usual. Went downstairs, got tea and then the telly. During the day I just went out to my mates and all.

Walking home, I saw Jessica's mam's car outside our house, which was very odd. I walked over to feel the front of the car to see was she here long. By the coldness of the car I knew she was. I had my key with me so I let myself in. Jessica was in the sitting room biting her bottom lip.

'What's wrong?' I said.

'I don't know,' she said. 'My mam just told me to get in the car and now we're here.'

Then we heard it. A knock on the door which was loud and strong, nearly putting the door through. I jumped up and went to answer it and there he was. The giant.

'Hello. Is your mother in?' he said in a deep tone of voice.

'Ehh…' I began, but before I could answer my mam had invited him into the kitchen for a cup of tea.

We tried to listen to the conversation that was going on in the kitchen with the giant but we couldn't hear anything. Then we heard someone moving so we ran and jumped on the sofa to act normal. Jessica's mam walked in and told us to come into the kitchen with her.

We were standing awkwardly in the kitchen, looking at the giant, who was sipping on a cup of tea. He put his cup down slowly and reached for something out of his pocket.

'I think this belongs to one of you,' he held up Jessica's phone.

I turned quickly to Jessica to see what she was going to say.

'Eh, yeah,' Jessica walked over to get it. 'Thanks,' she said, 'but how…'

'You left it in that back room yesterday,' the giant cut in. 'Oh, and my name is Mr Quinn by the way,' he raised his eyebrow. 'I thought I'd be nice and ring your mother's number and explain what happened, and arrange for me to return it,' he said with a sleazy smile. 'Now if you were so nice too,' he continued, 'you'd give me back that piece of paper you accidentally took when you were in our building,' he held his hand out.

I looked at my mam. She looked so confused. Just before she could say anything I pulled Jessica's jacket and I opened the front door and we ran.

'That was that thing you took yesterday,' I panted, 'what was it?'

'It's only a recipe for a cake,' she said. 'I wanted to make it so I took it.'

'You're a freak!' I shouted. 'You took a recipe when we were trying to run.'

'Where will we go?' said Jessica.

'Stephanie's,' I said. 'No one's in.'

When we reached Stephanie's house we knocked on the door

and followed Stephanie into her sitting room. I sat down beside her and explained what happened over the past two days and what we hoped to do there, which was make the cake.

At first she thought we were mad. Then she agreed and called her mam. I asked her if she had the ingredients and no surprise she did. We all went into the kitchen and began to bake a cake but after like ten minutes I felt tired.

'Here! I'm just going inside to lie down. Kinda tired now,' I said walking into the sitting room. As I fell onto the sofa I shouted, 'And if I fall asleep, wake me up when you're putting it into the oven, OK?'

I didn't hear a reply so I just took it as a yeah. Burying my head in the pillow I dozed off, falling into a nice dream.

'Becky! Becky!' I heard Stephanie in my ear as she pushed me back and forth. 'Eh, what?' I fell off the sofa. 'Ouch,' I said, holding my head because I'd hit the ground. 'What is it?' I said.

'The cake's ready for the heated hell,' she said, walking off. I think that was meant to be a joke. Stephanie was never good at them. I jumped up and fixed myself in the mirror before walking into the kitchen. Going into the kitchen I looked at the clock. Eleven o'clock. I couldn't help looking at the mess they'd made baking this cake.

'The mess in here! What were yous doing?' I said. 'Having a food fight, yeah?'

'No, it was hard, like, while you were asleep,' Stephanie said, while Jessica did her eyebrow thing.

I took the wooden spoon, then walked over and sat up on the table, licking the chocolate off.

'Did it take long?' I asked with chocolate around my mouth.

'Not that long, but long enough for you to start snoring,' said Jessica, laughing.

I laughed along with them, and asked how long it would take to bake the cake.

'Eh, about an hour or so,' said Stephanie. 'We can watch a film inside.'

I ran into the sitting room and got the most comfortable place.

Bang! Smack! Clash! A noise came from outside. I got Jessica to look out the window.

'Nothing there,' she said. 'Calm down!'

So we got back to the film. Fifty minutes passed.

'Right,' said Stephanie. 'Let's check this cake.'

We went into the kitchen and Jessica got the cake out of the oven while I got the plates and forks. We let the cake cool then dished it up.

'It tastes weird,' said Jessica. 'It doesn't taste the same as it usually does.'

Bang! Bang! Bang! Three loud knocks on the door.

Jessica and I kind of thought we knew who it was but we still didn't answer the door.

And of course we were right. It was the giant. He rushed in and went straight to the cake.

'So you made it,' he reached for the cake. 'That's nice. Now that you've made it and tasted it, can I please have the recipe back?'

Jessica looked at me. I nodded. She handed it over.

'Doesn't even taste the same,' she mumbled.

'Why's the recipe so important?' I asked the giant.

'Sorry, it's not for me to say,' the giant replied walking to the door. 'Enjoy your cake,' he turned at the door. 'Oh,' he said, 'and the reason it doesn't taste the same is because you didn't get the secret ingredient.'

'What secret ingredient?' Jessica asked.

'That's for me to know,' the giant said smartly.

We watched him leave.

The giant sat in his car outside and finished his piece of cake.

'It's good,' he said to himself, admiring the cake, 'but it would have been a lot nicer if they'd used the orange zest.'

Do It! Be Mad

Kirsty Hogan

Lucy doesn't live the life of a normal teenager. Lucy is from Lucan but has recently moved to Tallaght. Her mother got a new job at the Tallaght hospital and she felt it would be easier if they moved there. Tallaght is a very rough place to live in. Some parts are nice, but as for the rest—the less said the better.

Lucy is a nice girl, very kind and gentle. She's also very pretty: tall, skinny, with eyes so dark and big and her hair is so long. Lucy lives with her mother, her two sisters, Lindsey and Michelle, and her brother, Ben. Lucy's the youngest. Lucy's father was a big part of her life. He would take her to her football practices every day and on Sundays to her football matches. Her father moved to America when Lucy was just eight years old. She really misses him and would sometimes wonder if he's gone forever or if he will be back.

Ever since she was young, Lucy had been really close to her sister Lindsey. She had always talked about how Lindsey is an inspiration to her. Lindsey is a very kind-hearted girl, she works as a fashion designer and Lucy envies her. Lucy is a very lonely girl; she has no friends and constantly gets bullied at school. Everyone dislikes her for some reason and she just doesn't know why. Some teachers have told her it could be because she's a very private person, but Lucy doesn't agree with them as no one deserves to be bullied for any reason.

In fifth year Lucy joined the girls' football team; she really enjoys playing football and is very good and skillful. She recently got called up for the Ireland Under-17s. One time at training for the school team, the students started to bully her. A girl called Lauren is the leader of the bullies. She approached Lucy and said, 'Lucy why are you even here? The Miss said she hates you and you're not allowed play for this team anymore.'

'Why are you being so mean to me? Just leave me alone. The Miss would never say anything like that,' yelled Lucy. Just as Lucy turned her back, Lauren ran for her and pulled her hair.

Then the Miss rushed in. 'What's going on girls?' she screamed. No one replied, both girls kept their mouths shut!

'Oh yeah, Lucy, well done on making the Ireland team, you really deserved it.' Lucy's face lit up with excitement; as for Lauren, her face dropped with depression. She just held her head stiffly and stormed out of the room with a face on her like she was carrying the world on her shoulders. Lucy was really happy about making the Ireland team, but that excitement didn't change her life. She was being bullied and that's all that was on her mind, every minute of every day.

The bullying made her feel unwanted, unloved, hated and, worst of all, she felt like she wanted to be dead. Lucy didn't want to talk to anyone about it. She hoped since it was her last year of school the bullying would end. 'But then it won't end completely; it will be on my mind till the day I die,' Lucy thought sadly.

Lucy decided to talk to her mother. She told her mother about the problems at school, how she had no friends and how she was getting affected all of a sudden about her father.

'Do you not have any friends at school?' her mother asked in horror.

'No, no one likes me at school. I never want to go back there again!' Lucy screamed, with tears rolling down her face.

'Lucy, don't be saying that, everyone likes you. Why don't you go to the park and try to make friends?' her mother suggested.

'Mum, I'm sixteen, not five. I don't want to go to the park, only children go there!' said Lucy indignantly.

'Oh, Lucy, why don't you go to the shopping centre then, I'm sure you'll make friends there.'

'Mum, stop, just stop! I don't want to go to school, the park or the shopping centre,' said Lucy angrily.

'I'm just trying to help,' said Lucy's mother. 'Why don't you even try to make a few friends on the internet? My friend Ann at work recently told me that her daughter joined a thing called Bebo and made lots of friends.'

'Yeah, Mum, I've heard of it, but I don't think I'll make friends on it. However, I'll join it and see what it's like.'

'Great, Lucy, would you like me to help you set it all up?' asked Lucy's mother

'No, it's fine. I'll do it by myself. Thanks anyhow.'

'OK, Lucy, suit yourself.'

Lucy went straight upstairs and started to set up her Bebo account. She had to put all her details in, like her name and age. You had to be sixteen years old to join, but Lucy thought that if she put her age in as eighteen, she would make more friends. She did her Bebo page up, adding pictures, writing stuff about herself and finding a skin for her page. She added some random boys and girls she didn't know. Many of the people started texting her comments like, 'who is this?' and 'hey, you added me?' Lucy texted them back her name and that she was new to Bebo and just added them to make new friends. Soon after, she began having full conversations with all her Bebo friends. Lucy became addicted to Bebo and started joining other networking sites such as MSN, MySpace, Twitter, Facebook and Tagged. She made more and more friends on them as the days passed. Lucy was really happy and her mother noticed a big change in her.

'How's the Bebo thing getting on, did you make any new friends yet?' her mother asked.

'Oh yes, Mum, I've made loads of new friends,' Lucy replied.

'Really, that's wonderful, Lucy.'

'Yes, it is.'

Later that night, Lucy sat down at the table for dinner alongside her mother, her two sisters and her brother. Her mother told her sisters and her brother about Lucy making new friends on the internet; they were really happy for her. Since Lucy and her sister Lindsey were really close, they had a chat about it later and Lindsey told her to just be herself and have more confidence. The next day Lindsey took Lucy shopping and bought her lots of new clothes. Lucy looked really nice when she tried them on.

A few days later Lucy started chatting to two girls on Bebo, Sarah and Emily. They were really nice and kind to Lucy. Lucy knew they would be good friends just from texting them. They chatted on the internet for over two months before they arranged to go shopping one Sunday. When she met them in person they were really pretty. She immediately knew they would be real friends. Emily was the quiet one but was always happy. Sarah was wild, she suffered from ADHD. When Lucy told the girls about her getting bullied at school, Sarah began shouting, 'Ugh, I'm going to pull that Lauren's head off!'

But Lucy didn't want Sarah to start an argument so she calmed her down. Every Saturday the girls would go shopping and to the pictures and later, stay the night at one of the girls' houses together.

Lucy thought her life was going great, until bad news struck. One Wednesday night, she was at Sarah's house when she got a phone call from her mother. Her mother told her that her father has been in a serious car crash. Lucy couldn't cope with the pain. She just dropped the phone and ran out of Sarah's house crying hysterically. Sarah and Emily were baffled, so they phoned Lucy's mother and asked her. Her mother told them about Lucy's father and they ran after Lucy.

They found her in the park, crying her heart out, and tried to comfort her but she was in shock. Even though Lucy hadn't seen her father for over eight years, it still hurt her inside to know that the only person she ever looked up to was in a serious car crash. Lucy went home that night around nine o'clock and found her mother in the kitchen waiting with the phone in her left hand.

Lucy went to her crying and her mother gave her a big hug and said, 'Everything will be OK.'

Lucy nodded, taking her word. That night Lucy sat up praying that her father would be OK. She prayed so much that she fell asleep. Lucy woke up really late the next day. It was 12.40 p.m., too late for school. Her mother was at work so Lucy decided to get dressed and go into town for a while. In town she looked around the shops but no matter where she was or what shop she was in, the only thing that was on her mind was her father. Walking into one of the girly shops, a couple of girls approached her and asked her where she got her shoes; she told them her mother got them for her in America. She chatted to the girls for a little while. They were really nice. They told her to call them if she would like to hang out, so Lucy took their numbers and thought nothing more of it.

When she got home that evening, Lucy told her mother that she'd made a couple of new friends while at the shopping mall. Her mother was happy and encouraged her to call them. Kelly, one of the girls, asked Lucy if she would like to hang out with them over the weekend and Lucy said yes straight away. Lucy couldn't wait for the weekend to come. Her dad was still on her mind. Lucy prayed he would call, but though she prayed at least forty times a day, he never called.

Finally it was Saturday and Lucy's mother dropped her at the mall to meet the girls. When Lucy's mother saw them, she didn't like the look of them but Lucy was so excited that her mother didn't want to say anything. The girls hung around at the mall for a while before they got the bus into the city centre.

On the bus, Lucy looked out of the window at the people passing by. A girl walked down the street in a football kit and a bag on her shoulder and Lucy wondered if that would be her in the next few years. She saw a group of teenagers who were asleep on the side of the footpath and wondered why they lived like that and why they didn't have a home. 'Maybe they just don't have parents,' she thought, 'they may be lonely and depressed like me.' She kept staring out of the bus window while the other girls talked. All she could see were people and cars and more teenagers on the streets; Lucy felt so bad for them.

They went to a place called Temple Bar. It was dark out but this place was really bright and loud. There were lots of pubs and drunken people, people were singing out on the streets. Around the back was the Central Bank, with loads of underage drinkers and skateboarders. The place was full of tourists and tourist attractions. Lucy and the girls sat down on a little wall beside a group of boys and girls who were all really drunk. Lucy asked the girls why they were sitting with these people who were drinking alcohol. The other girl, Shannon, laughed and opened her hand bag. She took out a big litre of vodka and a packet of cigarettes.

'What in your right mind are you doing?' Lucy screamed.

'Ha ha, relax, Lucy,' the girls said.

Lucy sat down, quiet. The girls began to drink and smoke. They offered Lucy some but she refused.

'Lucy, when will you stop being a bore bag and just take some and be mad,' Kelly said.

'No, I don't want some,' Lucy replied.

'Why not? Just take some, everyone's doing it.'

'Yeah, but I'm not everyone,' Lucy answered.

'Lucy stop being boring. It's only this one time. It's not going to kill you. You should just take it and say thanks. After all, you're getting it for free,' they told Lucy.

Lucy thought for a moment: 'Should I? Or should I not?' Lucy was so stressed out, especially about her father, that she just said, 'OK give it here.' She drank it, the vodka! She drank so much that she could barely stand anymore. It was eleven o'clock and Lucy was supposed to be home. Her phone rang nonstop but she ignored it and turned it off, then went with the girls to a house party in Dun Laoghaire. At the party there were loads of people dancing, drinking and some were even taking drugs. Lucy was really drunk. She sat on a chair beside some boy and he asked if she was OK.

Lucy replied, 'Yeah, I'm grand, thanks.' The boy smiled and handed her a small bag with two tiny tablets in it.

'What are these for?' Lucy asked him, 'I told you I'm grand.'

'Ah no, you see, these small tablets, they make you feel great, they get you on a great buzz, just take them and I guarantee you you'll feel great. Go on, do it! Be mad!'

'Hmm, OK.' Pop, pop, Lucy took the tablets. Little did she know the tablets were E. Lucy started feeling really weird and out of her head, but in a way, it felt good. The girls walked in and saw Lucy. They told her she was one of them now and that she was mad. Lucy felt wanted but wondered if this was really who she wanted to be. Lucy stayed out all night. She knew her mother and her friends would be really worried about her but at this stage Lucy didn't care. The only person she cared about at this moment was herself. The next morning Lucy went home. She couldn't remember anything that happened the night before.

When she walked into her house her mother began to scream at her. 'Where were you last night, young lady?' her mother yelled.

Lucy thought of a quick excuse.

'Eh, eh, Mum, I'm so sorry but my phone went dead and I stayed at Kelly's house,' she replied.

'And may I ask who Kelly is?'

'She's one of my new friends,' said Lucy.

'Oh, I see, so since you've got these so-called new friends, you've forgotten your real friends Sarah and Emily.'

'No, Mum, it's not like that.'

'Oh yes, Lucy, it's exactly like that. I knew them girls were bad news the minute I seen them,' said Lucy's mother angrily.

'What do you mean? They are good friends.'

'No, Lucy, they are not and the quicker you figure that out the better. Just go to your room. You're grounded!'

'Ugh, OK, I'm going.'

Lucy went upstairs to her room. Her father still hadn't called and she felt really upset. She picked her phone off the table, put her jacket on and climbed out her window. She felt so sick of her life she didn't care what anyone thought of her anymore.

Lucy decided to run away from home. She phoned the girls, Kelly, Shannon, Chloe and Jenny, then jumped on the bus to meet them in town. They told her she was really cool to run away from home and Lucy felt like one of them; she felt mad. That night, the girls all got drunk and went to another party. Just as they were entering the party, Lucy's phone started to ring. It was her mother but Lucy ignored the phone calls.

Once again Lucy drank too much alcohol, took some tablets and smoked some kind of drug. The drug was really strong and she didn't know what she was doing anymore, she was so out of her head. Her phone rang constantly; her whole family was out looking for her. There was a text message left on her phone from Emily, 'Lucy where re ye? what has gotten into ye? Y re ye doing this? Please jus ring one of us, let us no your safe!'

Lucy threw her phone over the back wall and ignored the text message. She didn't want to go home tonight; she didn't want to go home ever again! She had nowhere to stay for the night so she ended up staying out on the street with one of the boys from the party. It was really cold. Lucy remembered that Saturday when she was on the bus looking out of the window at the teenagers sleeping on the side of the footpath and thought, 'I'm doing the same thing now. I don't know why I'm doing something so dangerous like staying out on the streets all night with a stranger.'

Days passed. Lucy was now homeless, all because of one stupid mistake. Addicted to drugs and alcohol, Lucy was now one of them. She had left behind her family, friends and even school. She lived on the streets, in corners and in doorways, under small pieces of cardboard with no food or money. Her family and friends didn't want to know her anymore and her life was basically turned upside down.

With no money to feed her bad habits of alcohol and drug abuse, Lucy began shoplifting and snatching bags, stealing money and valuables from people. She got arrested nearly every day for the same things: stealing, drinking and also for being caught with drugs. Days and months passed and her condition worsened. Her life was now really horrible and scary.

Two years later on a cold winter night, Sarah and Emily were on a walk in town when a young girl approached them.

'Sorry, you wouldn't be able to spare me a bit of change would you?' she begged.

Sarah and Emily looked at each other in shock and Sarah grabbed the girl's hand. 'Lucy! Oh my God, Lucy,' she screamed.

'What do you think you're doing touching me? Get your hands off me now,' Lucy shouted.

'Lucy?'

'Yeah, how do you know my name?'

'Oh my God, Lucy, it's us—Sarah and Emily.'

Lucy thought for a few minutes then broke down into tears.

'You are my friends, you're my friends,' she sobbed.

'Yes, we are. What have you done to yourself, Lucy?'

'I don't know, I just don't know. It was parties, boys, drink, drugs, living on the streets, I just don't know.'

'Lucy, don't worry, we're here for you, so is your whole family. Your father is back from America, he pulled through the accident.'

Lucy's face lit up. Sarah and Emily called Lucy's mother and told her that they had found Lucy and she was coming home. What her mother didn't know was that her daughter was a drug addict and alcoholic. When Lucy's mother saw her, she was devastated and heartbroken. Lucy's family decided to get her help. They came together, as did her friends. It wasn't easy but Lucy was willing and determined to put in the time. Lucy soon became stronger and after a year and a half of treatment centres and rehabs, Lucy was drug and alcohol free. For her fresh start, Lucy went for a new hairstyle and got new clothes to celebrate her new life.

Lucy was twenty-one when she decided to go back to school to finish her Leaving Cert, then she moved on to college to get a degree for teaching business. She spent four years in college. While at UCD, Lucy met a man, Colm. They fell in love and five years later the two got married and had twins, Kaitlin and Adam.

By the age of thirty-two, Lucy has a new husband, twins, two best friends and the best family you could ask for. She is now a fully-qualified teacher and has gone back to playing football, this time professionally. And there's more: Lucy is also a part-time clothing model for her sister Lindsey and they both get to travel the world together.

All those people that bullied her at school, the people who had her doing bad things and the people she was living on the streets with, they don't matter anymore. They were a part of Lucy's old life that is now forgotten and that's the reason why they didn't make it into her future.

When Love Takes Over

Marian Ivanov

Ever wonder what teenagers do in school nowadays?

This is the story of a boy called Jim who fell for a new girl named Sally. It begins on a sunny Monday morning when Jim was upstairs in his room, listening to Spin 103.8 and getting ready for his first day back at school.

Jim heard on the radio that there was a competition for two free tickets to go and see Britney Spears live at the O2. He listened carefully to the question, so he could enter the draw to see the star on September 17th.

The question was, 'When is Britney's birthday? A: 8th December, B: 2nd December, C: 3rd December or D: 9th December.'

Jim knew the answer, of course, and texted it as quickly as possible to Spin 103.8.

'Jim,' his mum called up the stairs. 'It's 8.30 now. Come on, you don't want to be late.'

Jim put on his shoes and ran downstairs. 'Bye, Mum,' he said.

'Bye, son, have a wonderful day.'

On his way to school, Jim heard the message tone on his phone.

He had a new message. From Spin 103.8.

'Congrats lucky texter! Now we need your name and address so we can put you in the draw to see Britney live.'

Jim grinned. He quickly typed his name and address and sent the text. Then he turned off his phone, because you had to before you entered the school building. That was a law all students had to obey.

In class, he saw the new girl, Sally. The minute he saw her he knew it was too good to be true. He felt love.

At break time, Jim walked over to Sally and asked her, 'What age are you?'

Sally looked at him weirdly, and said, 'I'm fifteen.'

Jim was puzzled and wondered why she wasn't asking him his age. 'Why is she not asking me my age, hmmm'—that was in his brain.

There was also a girl called Jane in Jim's class. She was the same height as Jim and wore glasses, and she pulled Sally away from Jim, dragging her by her blonde hair. Jim didn't think this was a good idea. And he was right.

Jim had a true friend named Sam. Sam was also in Jim's class and he was also confused about Sally's behaviour.

After school, Jim went to talk to Sally but she said, 'GET AWAY!'

Going home, Jim was not in a happy mood.

'Hey, son, how was school?' his mum asked. 'You don't seem to be very happy.'

'Love stinks,' Jim said.

'Aww, what happened today? Tell me, son.'

'Well, this new girl I like, she's mean to me,' Jim said. 'Thanks to that girl, Jane, with the glasses, my life has gone from happy to sad.'

'Don't worry, I'm sure there is a mystery behind all this,' his mum said.

'So, how do I solve the mystery?'

'Well, if I were you, I would act like her and see what happens when you ignore her.'

'Mum, you are a genius,' Jim said.

He ran upstairs, called Sam and asked him to come over to his house.

An hour later, the doorbell rang.

'Hey, Sam, what's up?' Jim said.

'Nothing much, just played the PlayStation,' Sam said.

Jim and Sam went upstairs.

'So, why did you want me to come over?' Sam asked.

'I got a plan,' Jim said.

'A plan for what, Jim?'

'To solve the mystery about Sally's behaviour towards us,' Jim said.

'And how will we do that?'

'By pretending we don't see her in class.'

'Oh, I see, so then she will start talking to us?' Sam asked curiously.

'Yes, now you get me,' Jim said.

Jim and Sam watched *Zoey 101* for two hours. Jim's mum came in with pizza and two orange drinks. 'Here, have some food, boys,' she said.

'Thanks,' Sam and Jim said.

The next day, back in Jim's house, the boys talked some more.

'I have bad news about Sally,' Sam said. 'She is being a real bitch.'

'Yes I know she is,' Jim said.

Sam put on the radio. 'What can we do about it?'

Jim heard his name on the radio.

'Our finalists are Tara, Jim, Fred and Kate,' the Spin 103.8 presenter said.

'Wow,' Jim said.

'Tara, Jim, Fred and Kate, next week we will call the winner of the tickets to the Britney Spears Circus Tour at the O2.'

'Sam, did you hear that?'

'Yes I did, Jim.'

'I'm happy now. I can't wait till next week.'

'I've got a plan,' Sam said.

'For what?'

'For Sally.'

'OK, go on, tell me.'

'Maybe she's too shy to talk to you.'

'Dude, I don't get you. You said you have a plan. What do you mean too shy to talk to me?'

'Listen, you big buffalo, I think you are better off forgetting about her,' Sam said.

'Wow, dude, you are a pain in the back of my head,' Jim said.

'I'm only trying to help.'

'No, dude, you are trying to make me forget about her. Why?'

'I never said that,' Sam said nervously.

'Yes, you did. Are you keeping something from me?'

'Nope.'

'Why are you going red then?'

'Emmmm, don't know,' Sam said.

'Let me guess.'

'Guess what?'

'You are going out with her.'

'No I am not!' Sam shouted and left.

Next day in school, Jim and Sam spoke to each other again.

'Hey, pal.'

'Hey, dude, sorry about yesterday, thinking that you're with her.'

'It's OK.'

They had PE first class. They did press-ups, sit-ups and pull-ups. Once again, they ignored Sally. But Sally still wouldn't talk to them.

After school, Sam told Jim he couldn't go to his house.

'Why not?' Jim asked.

'A family thing. See you tomorrow, bud,' Sam said while stepping away from Jim.

Jim decided to go to town and get some clothes he had seen the week before in Champion Sports. He saw Sally and Sam in town. They were in a romantic restaurant. Kissing.

Jim got so angry that he went home and took a cold shower to calm himself down.

'OH MY GOD,' he said to himself.

'OH MY GOD,' he said again, shivering.

He went for a walk in the forest near him to get some fresh air after his horrible day. He walked slowly, liking the fresh air. Suddenly, he tripped over something. He looked down and saw a dusty old lamp, hard as metal, on the ground. He picked it up and cleared away the dust. Everything around him went grey. He coughed while the grey dust cleared.

Just then, he saw a blue genie. He was shocked. He thought genies only appeared in stories.

'Hello there, young boy. I'm a magical genie. I can make your wishes come true,' Genie of the lamp said.

'I didn't think genies existed,' Jim said.

'We do exist. Otherwise, would I be in front of you now?' Genie of the Lamp said.

'I guess you are real, but do you have a name or will I just call you Genie Of The Lamp?' Jim asked, calming down.

'My name is Boris, and what is your name, boy?'

'It's Jim. So can I make wishes, Boris?'

'Sure you can, but only three, so use them wisely.'

'Excellent,' Jim said.

'Yes, but you have to sign a contract to make sure you get what you ask for because sometimes not everything comes true,' Boris said, taking a contract from the tree near him.

'Cool,' Jim said.

Boris gave him a black pen, also from the tree. Jim signed the contract. Boris clicked his fingers and the sheet of paper flew into the lamp.

'So, can I keep you?' Jim asked.

'Yes, I belong to you until you've got your three wishes. Whenever you need me, just clap your hands twice.'

Jim took the lamp home with him and, later that night, decided to make a wish. He clapped his hands twice.

Boris came out of the lamp. 'Yes, Jim. What's up?'

'Hey, Boris, I think I have a wish for you.'

'I hear you, Jim.'

'I would like to wish—'

'Sorry to interrupt you, but you need to start off by saying, "O mighty Genie, I would like to wish for blah blah bla." Get it?'

But before Jim could say anything, the house went pitch black. A few seconds later, the lights came back on.

'What did you do?' Jim asked.

'I didn't do anything,' Boris said.

It went dark again.

'Enough jokes, Genie,' Jim said.

'It's not me,' Boris replied.

The lights came back on. A pink girl genie appeared. 'Hello hello,' she said.

'Hi,' Jim and Boris said at the same time.

'My name is Amanda, the pink genie. I know more about love than any genie in the world.'

'So, why are you here?' Jim asked.

'Because I hear you have girl troubles,' Amanda said.

'Quite true,' Jim said.

'And you found my cousin, Boris,' Amanda said.

'He's your cousin? Wow, I didn't know that,' Jim said, shocked.

'It's true,' Boris said.

'Cool, is this like winning the jackpot?' Jim laughed.

'Oh yeah, it's like winning a million euro,' Amanda said. 'Now that you have me, I'll stay by your side and help you out in life. If you want that girl, Sally, you have to get to be Nadia's friend, Kate. Nadia is Sally's sister and Kate is Nadia's best friend. You will have a chance to be Kate, and if you really love Sally, it will work. If you don't, then this is all a waste of time.'

'Wow, you'll really do that for me? I don't know what to say,' Jim said.

Just then, he heard his mum and dad coming up the stairs. 'Quick, hide in the lamp,' he said.

The genies hid.

'We heard you speaking with some girl,' Jim's mum said.

'Nobody's here, Mum,' Jim said.

'We're sure we heard you with someone,' his mum said.

'Maybe he's just here with a nice girl and we should give them a bit of space,' Jim's dad said. 'Come on, honey, *Desperate Housewives*.'

Jim's parents went back to the living room.

'Phew,' Jim said and clapped twice.

'Are they gone?' Boris asked.

'Yeah, but we have to speak quietly so they don't hear us talking,' Jim said.

'OK,' Amanda said.

'Thanks for understanding,' Jim said.

'Jim, whenever you're ready to be transformed into Kate, you tell me, OK?' Amanda said with a smile.

'OK, but not now,' Jim said. 'I've got to go to bed. I found two genies today, so I think I need to sleep.'

At school the next day, everything was OK between Jim and Sam —on the surface at least.

'What's up buddy?' Sam asked.

'Ah, nothing much, just had a bad day yesterday,' Jim said.

'Oh, why?'

'It doesn't matter now.' Jim remained calm, but he felt like giving Sam a big punch in the face.

'I can't come to your house for two weeks,' Sam said. 'My mum says I have to study.'

'Cool, you have fun studying,' Jim said.

Later, when he was back home, he clapped his hands twice.

'Hey genies, I want to be turned into Kate,' he said.

'As you wish, but there's something you can't do when you are Kate,' Amanda said.

'What can I not do?'

'When you are Kate, you cannot speak to Sally,' Amanda explained. 'If you do, you'll turn back into Jim. While you're the fake Kate, the real Kate will be hypnotised; she won't be on Earth, she'll be on Mars.'

'Cool, I'm ready,' Jim said.

'Get as much information from Nadia as you can,' Boris said.

Amanda took a potion from her cousin's lamp and gave it to Jim. 'Once you drink this, you will be at Nadia's door, ringing her bell. Remember, don't talk to Sally about anything.'

Jim drank the potion and before he knew it, he was at Nadia's door ringing the doorbell.

'Hey, Kate,' Nadia said.

'Hey, Nadia, how are you keeping?' Kate asked.

They went upstairs to Nadia's room, and Nadia showed Kate her new poster of Tupac.

'Wow, did you buy this today?' Kate asked.

'Yeah, isn't it a great poster?'

Kate laughed for a few seconds. 'It's super, but why do you have a poster of him?'

'Why? Kate, are you out of your mind?'

'No.'

'Yes, you are. Do you not remember that I'm his biggest fan?'

'Of course, I remember,' Kate said. 'But why do you have pictures of Britney Spears too?'

'OH MY GOD, you have gone mad in your head. Are you sure you're feeling OK?'

'I'm feeling good.'

'Then why don't you remember that I'm Britney's fan too?'

Jim tried to think of an excuse. 'Uh, I forgot, ha,' Kate said.

'How could you forget, Kate?' Nadia asked curiously.

'OK, OK, I hit my head in PE class today,' Kate said, trying to put on a sad face.

Nadia smiled. 'Kate, you should have told me. Why didn't you tell me?'

'I didn't want you to know, sorry, girl,' Kate said.

Nadia hugged Kate.

'Nadia, can I ask you a few questions about your sister, Sally?' Kate said.

'Sure,' Nadia said with a smile.

They talked nearly all night.

When Jim got home, Amanda turned him back to himself.

'Genies, today was the best day,' he said.

'Why was it the best day?' Boris asked.

'Because I got to know lots of stuff I never knew.'

'Like?' both genies said.

'Well, I got to know that Sally likes when I'm singing to her.'

'Cool. Did you know that tomorrow on the radio they will announce the winner of the Britney Spears Concert?' Amanda asked.

'I'd forgotten about that,' Jim said. 'But how did you know I have a chance to win?'

'We looked through your message inbox,' Boris said.

Jim smiled. 'Well, thanks for reminding me.'

The following day, Jim sang so that Sally would notice him. Sam noticed Sally looking at Jim more than ever. He couldn't take it anymore, so he went over to Jim.

'What the hell are you up to?' he said. 'She's my girlfriend.'

'I know she is,' Jim said in a mad tone of voice.

'Then back off or I'll punch the head off you.'

'You would, yeah right,' Jim said, getting ready to fight him.

'Have it your way. Me and you—after school fight,' Sam said.

'Fine, see you there, loser.'

Over three hundred students turned up to see Jim and Sam fight in the park. There was a huge circle around the boys. Jim pretended to kick Sam but instead threw a punch and Sam fell on his back. Sam got up quickly and pretended to punch Jim in the face. Instead, he kicked him so hard that Jim fell like a crisp falling from the Spire.

'Hahaha, who is on the floor now?' Sam said.

'What kind of friend are you? After all the things I done for you,' Jim said, trying to get up.

'Shut up, you. You've never done anything good for me,' Sam said, kicking Jim even harder.

The other three hundred students just recorded the fight on their phones. No one tried to help Jim.

During the fight, the school principal arrived in the park. 'RIGHT, WHAT THE HELL IS GOING ON HERE?' he shouted.

He saw Jim lying on the ground. He also knew that Sam had started the fight. 'SAM, COME HERE NOW!'

Sam walked over to the principal.

'DO YOU REALISE WHAT YOU ARE DOING?'

'Yes, I'm sorry but he started it,' Sam said.

'Right, you two, see me in my office at once,' the principal said.

Sam and Jim went to the principal's office.

'Well, Sam, I hear you were the one who started the fight,' the principal said.

'No, that's bullshit, sir,' Sam said.

'Mind your language, young man.'

'Sorry, sir.'

'Sam, I've had enough of your messing. You need to learn manners, so, for the rest of the term, you will stay back after school and clean each classroom. If you decide not to do this, well, you might as well get out of the school. You also need to say sorry to Jim.'

'Sorry, Jim, and I will do as you say, sir, but promise me you won't tell my mum, sir,' Sam said.

'I don't forgive him, sir, I can't forgive such a backstabber. He should feel my pain,' Jim said.

'Jim won't forgive you and he's right. Now, you two, get out of my office and if I ever hear of you in a fight again I'll make your lives a living hell,' the principal said.

At home, Jim clapped twice.

'Jim, did you know that the winner is about to be announced on the radio?' Boris said.

'I had forgotten about that. I was in a fight today with Sam,' Jim said.

'I knew something bad would happen. Are you OK now?'

Amanda asked.

'I'm fine, thanks. I'll put the radio on,' Jim said.

He put on the radio and listened carefully.

'Now it's time for the winner of the Britney tickets. The winner will be called after the new Britney song, "3".'

'Who'll be the winner?' Jim asked.

'Kate,' Boris said.

'So, can I be transformed into Kate?' Jim asked.

'OK, you will turn into Kate in three, two, one,' Amanda replied.

'Now it's time for everyone to hear who the winner is,' the Spin 103.8 presenter said.

'Remember, bring Nadia with you to the concert,' Boris said.

'I will,' Jim said.

'The winner is Kate,' the presenter said.

Kate's phone rang. 'Hello,' she said.

'Hi, is this Kate?' the presenter asked.

'Yeah.'

'Do you know why I'm ringing you?'

'Is it for the Circus concert?'

'Yes, it is.'

'Cool,' Kate said.

Kate called Nadia. 'Nadia, I'll be coming to your house today,' she said happily.

'Cool, I'll be waiting for you,' Nadia said.

At Nadia's house, Kate told her about winning the tickets. Nadia said she couldn't go to the concert but that her sister Sally would go instead.

Sally came down from her room, smiling.

'Why are you so happy?' Nadia asked.

'I broke up with my boyfriend,' Sally said.

'No way, sister. I'm proud of you,' Nadia said.

Kate was very happy that Sally was single because it meant Sally could now be Jim's girlfriend.

Sally dressed well for the concert. She wore a sexy, colourful jumper with light blue jeans and red boots.

At the concert, Britney landed on stage in a parachute and began to sing her song 'Sometimes'.

Jim felt the love when the song was on, and, just then, he heard Sally say, 'This is how I feel about Jim.'

He was so happy to hear it from Sally's lips.

'Aww, you two should go out,' Kate said.

Jim remembered that he should have not spoken to Sally, but it was too late. He transformed back to himself.

Sally turned to get her drink and saw Jim beside her. 'AAAAAAHHH,' she yelled.

'Chill, chill, please chill,' Jim said.

'How can I chill? You were Kate. That's freaky!' Sally shouted.

'Wait, I can explain,' Jim said.

'No you can't. What's wrong with you?' Sally asked.

'You have no idea what I have been through,' Jim said.

'Do I not? Well, I know you totally freaked me out.'

'I'm sorry.'

'Sorry? Are you joking me, are you?'

'Can I tell you the truth?'

'Go on before I snap,' Sally said, calming down.

'All these things I did, I did because I love you,' Jim said.

'That is the nicest thing anyone has ever done for me,' Sally said, happily.

'And it's all true,' Jim said.

'I love you, Jim, you are the greatest thing that could happen to me,' Sally said.

They left the Britney concert and went to Jim's house. Jim wanted to show Sally the genies. He clapped twice.

'Hello, you must be Sally,' Boris said.

'Yeah, that's me,' Sally said.

'My name is Boris and we are magical genies that care for Jim.'

'My name is Amanda.'

'How did you find them, Jim?' Sally asked.

'Well, it's a long story. Let's just say it was like magic,' Jim said.

'If they are real genies, can I make a wish?' Sally asked.

'Sure you can,' Amanda said.

'I wish that Kate would come back to her original life,' Sally said.

'Your wish is my command, my lady,' Boris said.

'Now we can wish for whatever we want and live happily ever after with each other,' Jim said.

Never give up on the one you love, even if magic can't help you. From that day forward, all the characters lived happily ever after. Nadia, Sally's sister was delighted for Jim and Sally, but she never found out the magic behind it all.

Friendship

Natalina Marcella

It all started on her first day back to school. Three months after spending most of the summer holidays in Italy with relatives, Bianca had a nice new hairstyle—dark and shiny with a funky cut. She couldn't wait to see her best friend Jessica and catch up with what had happened while they were apart. They were both so excited to be seniors now. When they saw each other they ran up to each other and hugged.

'Hey, how are you?' Bianca said. 'Oh my God! You've changed.'

'I know,' Jessica replied. 'I love your hair, Bianca, and your skin is so tanned. I wish I was you.'

They both had so much to tell each other they didn't know where to start. But they knew a place.

Barcode. Where else would they be on a Wednesday night? Suddenly, they saw Jasmine, a member of their class, who always thought she was better than everyone else. She was dancing with a group of boys that they liked.

Jessica and Bianca went over and tried to talk and dance with Jasmine and the boys but Jasmine was not sharing. Knowing that Bianca and Jessica were watching, Jasmine gobsmacked one of the boys that Jessica liked but the girls pretended not to notice. They just turned around and walked away and mixed with some other friends they knew. Later on Bianca and Jessica tried to go back dancing with the boys but the boys didn't want them to, so

they kind of pushed them away. The girls felt mortified. But they got over it and at one point they were messing, throwing each other into fellas they liked. But when Bianca got pushed into the boy she fancied, he just kept walking. He didn't respond to her which made her feel hurt inside but she wouldn't show it. She was used to being made feel like that because it was something Jessica did all the time.

When Barcode ended, the girls were standing outside waiting on a taxi to head off home when one of the boys that Jessica liked said:

'Free gaff. Ya comin?'

'Hold on. I'll ask me friend,' said Bianca. 'Jessica, do you want ta?'

'I don't know,' said Jessica, 'you know the way my parents are. They won't trust us.'

So, of course, they went. Everything got a bit wild. Jessica was having loads of fun but for some reason Bianca wasn't. Nobody knew what was wrong with her.

Jessica was all over the place, dancing and meeting everyone but this boy, David, asked her to go up to a room, so she went with him.

By now everyone was drunk. They were drinking beer and lots of WKD.

David whispered into Jessica's ear what he'd like to do next. She thought to herself: 'I've gone this far. Why not?'

Half an hour later, David and Jessica came back downstairs to the party. Jessica was scared to tell Bianca what had happened. She searched everywhere for Bianca and finally found her standing on her own, just listening to the music with a worried look on her face.

'Thank God, Jess. Where were you? I was getting worried,' Bianca said.

Jessica told her what had happened. Bianca didn't know what to say or think. She just stood there in shock, feeling both glad and jealous.

'What will my parents think if they find out?' Jessica asked. 'What will happen if everyone in school finds out?'

'Don't mind what people in school think or say,' said Bianca. 'It's none of their business, but can I ask you something Jessica? Do you even know him?'

Jessica started to cry.

'No, I don't even know him,' she cried, 'but I didn't want him to think I was a chicken or a nerd.'

'Don't cry,' Bianca hugged her. 'Everything will be OK,' she said, only half believing it herself, but saying anything just to calm her friend down.

The party ended very late and they ended up sleeping on the floor in the sitting room. Then the next morning they got up before everyone else and went to the nearest bus stop. It was still early in the morning so they decided to treat themselves to a McDonalds.

They went along Stephen's Green and walked around town for a while because they were bored and they wanted to kill some time and think of what they were going to tell their parents.

Suddenly Bianca said: 'Oh my God, look at that stunner over there. He's gorgeous. Let's try and get his digits.'

'Oh my God,' said Jessica, 'I'm talking about something serious and you're looking at fellas. Could you not be sensible for one minute?'

'Sorry,' said Bianca, 'but he's gorgeous.'

So Jessica, knowing that Bianca was not paying attention said: 'Where? What fella?'

'Over there!' Bianca replied.

'Oh yeah,' said Jessica, 'he is nice. Jesus, Bianca you've great eyesight,' she sighed.

Bianca laughed, all giddy.

'Well, when it comes to fellas, always. Ha ha.'

'Excuse me,' the two girls shouted.

The nice boy turned around and said, 'Who me?'

'Yeah, you,' said the girls, laughing.

'You're massive,' said Jessica.

'Yeah, you're a beaut,' said Bianca.

The boy stood there in shock.

'Thanks,' he said.

A girl came over. She looked like Paris Hilton.

'Who are you?' she sneered at Jessica.

'Who the fuck are you? Have ya got a problem, bitch?' answered Jessica.

'Leave her, Jess. She's not worth it,' said Bianca.

Jessica looked at the Paris Hilton lookalike again, then as she was walking away, she gave her a dirty look and said to the boy, 'I think you're too good for that yoke beside ya.'

Then Jessica and Bianca linked each other and walked away laughing, leaving the boy confused and the girl in shock.

When they got home Bianca's mum was really mad at both of them. Bianca was grounded for two months and she wasn't allowed to speak to Jessica anymore. Jessica just got an earbashing from her parents because she was an only child.

Even though Bianca was forbidden to speak to Jessica or hang around with her she didn't obey her parents' orders, but when she next saw Jessica, her friend was very edgy and nervous. Jessica told Bianca that she didn't get her time of the month and she was very worried.

Jessica had never told anyone else what had happened that night at the party. Only Bianca knew. One day when she went into school Jessica started hearing all these rumours that she was pregnant, then one of the girls came up to her and said: 'Is it true that you might be pregnant?'

The only person Jessica was certain knew anything was Bianca and the guy from the party, of course, but at this stage she couldn't even remember his name. Jessica asked the girl who had told her she might be pregnant.

'Bianca, but don't say I told you,' said the girl.

Jessica got so annoyed she raced around the school looking for Bianca. When she found her Bianca was laughing and joking, but Jessica's eyes were full of tears.

'What the fuck is going on, Bianca?' said Jessica. 'Is it true?'

'It wasn't me. I swear,' said Bianca.

'How could you?' said Jessica. 'I trusted you. I thought you were my best friend. You're like a sister to me. Why did you say it to everyone?'

Bianca knew in her heart she had made a big mistake so she said: 'I can see you're upset. Look, I only told Ashleigh because she asked had I any news.'

'You told her my business,' said Jessica. 'How could you? I'd never do that to you. You know she's a big mouth. You filled her mouth with my private life and now look what's happened.'

Bianca felt like shit and it only hit her there and then what opening her mouth had done to their friendship. She said with tears in her eyes: 'I'm so sorry, Jessica. I just didn't know what to do, or say, or how to help you.'

They both started to cry and hugged each other. Both of them wanted to know the truth—if Jessica was pregnant or not—so Bianca went and got a pregnancy test for her and it turned out she wasn't. Jessica was so relieved; they both were but they did one more test just in case. It came out the same so she definitely wasn't having a baby.

Jessica learned a few lessons from this: to never ever do any thing just to be cool and to walk away from something in future if she didn't know what she was doing and friendship is something that cannot be taken for granted. It's a good friend that will always try to put good things in your head and always listen to good advice.

Crossing Over
Amanda Miller

The alarm went off, ringing like mad.

'Err,' she groaned.

It was another typical Monday morning. As Laura crawled out of bed she thought something was missing in her life. A little excitement. In school Laura and the rest of her friends were talking about what they wanted to do after their Leaving Cert.

'I'd love to go and work in America. I hear a lot of exciting stuff happens there,' Laura announced.

'Nah. I'd like a challenge,' said Taylor.

Laura guessed what she was going to say.

'Egypt,' said Taylor.

'OK, it's a deal,' said Laura

So the two girls agreed they'd go to Egypt. That night Taylor went on her computer to book the tickets but before she knew it, she'd made a mistake and booked a one-way flight to Italy.

'Dammit,' she thought to herself.

The next day when Taylor told Laura about the computer error Laura went mad but then shortly snapped out of it. To be honest she seemed a bit excited about the mistake.

The months dragged by. The Leaving Cert finally came and went. The girls were excited to go on their holidays, to a new place filled with interesting people and a different language. The flight was long and boring but when they got to Italy there was music playing and people singing and dancing outside restaurants.

'This is fantastic, isn't it?' Laura shouted over the noise.

'Yeah! It's fabulous,' Taylor shouted back.

The girls headed to their hotel. Taylor loved a bit of a mystery so she had booked the two of them into a really old hotel that was said to be haunted. When they were settled in their room Taylor and Laura decided to go for a swim. They were in the locker room when Taylor jumped with shock.

'Taylor, what's wrong?' said Laura.

Taylor didn't reply. Her eyes were wide with shock.

'Taylor! Stop it, you're scaring me,' said Laura.

'Sorry,' said Taylor, 'it's just that I saw someone going out the door.'

Laura got a really chilling feeling down her back, but she pretended not to be scared. 'Oh, don't be silly. People walk in and out of here all the time. It could have been one of the staff.'

Taylor shook her head. 'It was a ghost-like figure, Laura, fleeing out through those doors,' she pointed at the entrance to the locker room.

The two girls got into the pool trying to forget what had happened, but Taylor couldn't get the image of the figure out of her head.

That night, as she lay in bed, Taylor heard crying coming from one of the rooms. 'I wonder who could be up at this hour,' she thought.

Taylor put on her dressing gown, tip-toed past Laura who was sound asleep, and followed the crying noise, down the corridor. Arriving at Room 220, she pushed the door open, and was shocked to see the ghost-like figure she'd seen earlier, sitting in the rocking chair singing. It was a girl, a beautiful girl in a long white dress. Taylor stood and stared in silence for a moment or two. The singing sounded like wind chimes, so peaceful. As Taylor stood and watched, the girl turned and saw her. She stood up and reached out for Taylor's hand.

'Laura! Laura!' Taylor screamed. Turning quickly, she ran back to their room, and jumped on her sleeping friend's bed.

'What? What! What is it?' Laura was angry at being woken from her sleep. 'Why did you wake me?' she said, annoyed.

'Sorry, sorry, Laura, but I have something to tell you, and I know you won't believe me,' Taylor said, out of breath, 'but it's true, it really is.'

'What? What is it?' Laura rubbed her eyes.

'I was lying in bed when I heard someone crying,' said Taylor. 'So I followed it down the corridor to Room 220, but as I opened the door I saw a ghost, the same ghost I saw down by the pool today. And, Laura, she was sitting in a chair and she was singing...' Taylor broke off as she tried to make sense of it.

'Well, it could be one of the staff cleaning the room,' said Laura.

'No!' said Taylor. 'Why would the staff clean at four in the morning? And besides, she was wearing a dress, a long white dress, like a wedding dress!' said Taylor.

'Mmm. Well, whatever it was, it can wait till morning,' Laura pulled the covers back over her head.

The next morning Taylor went to the hotel archives to see if she could find out more about the room and the girl.

'Weddings,' she muttered to herself. 'I need to see who got married in this hotel.'

It didn't take long to find what she was looking for.

'Laura! Laura, look at this!' she shouted.

'What?' Laura looked up from the file she was reading.

'It says here that a girl killed herself at her wedding in this hotel,' Taylor showed Laura a newspaper clipping with a photo of the girl she had seen singing in Room 220.

'It was years ago.' Laura pointed at the date on the top of the newspaper article. 'Why would she still be hanging around? Haunting the place? Scaring people like you and me?'

'Her name was Sabrina,' said Taylor, looking down at the photograph of the girl.

'Come on.' She tugged on Laura's sleeve. 'We have to find her and see if we can help her.'

'Why?' said Laura, 'and how? How can we help her?'

'If she's still here after all these years' said Taylor, 'there's a reason. It means she can't cross over; she can't get to where she wants to go, because something hasn't been sorted here. There's something here she needs to sort before she can move on.'

The two girls went back to Room 220. Taylor turned the light on. The light flickered, then went off again.

'Sabrina,' said Taylor. 'Are you here? Can you tell us what happened you?'

'No,' said a voice, 'but I can show you.'

An overwhelming feeling came over Taylor. She felt her eyes close, then open again, and suddenly she saw Sabrina standing in front of her, crying as she put a beautiful heart-shaped locket into a pale pink box with little turquoise diamonds on the sides. Taylor watched Sabrina hide the pink box under the floorboards. Taylor jerked, then blinked as she came out of the trance but found herself immediately slipping into another one where she felt hands around her neck, choking her. Squeezing tight. She couldn't breathe. Taylor panicked and passed out. When she came to, Laura was standing over her.

'Tay? Are you okay? What happened?' Laura looked worried.

Taylor sat up.

'We have to help her,' she said.

'Who?' said Laura.

'Sabrina,' said Taylor. 'Come on!'

Taylor took Laura by the hand and dragged her back to Room 220. As soon as they walked in Laura got a chilling feeling down her spine.

'Taylor, I want to wait outside.'

'Oh, don't be such a baby,' said Taylor.

'No! I can't!' said Laura. 'I'm scared.'

'OK, wait outside,' said Taylor. 'You can keep your eye out for any hotel staff.'

Taylor went into Room 220 and felt a little nervous because she didn't know what might happen.

'Sabrina?' said Taylor, 'are you here? I know you're angry at whoever did this to you but I'm a friend. I'm here to help you cross over.'

'No!' came the voice. 'I'm not going until he gets it.' Sabrina sounded as if she was about to cry.

'Why?' said Taylor. 'Why can't you just go into the light? Cross over? You will be much better there. You can see all your family' Taylor was almost about to cry herself.

'I won't see all of my family. I have to get it to him.' Sabrina wasn't making sense.

'Why are you stuck?' asked Taylor.

Sabrina didn't respond.

'Please,' said Taylor, 'please tell me. I want to help you.'

'OK,' said Sabrina after a long pause. 'I'll tell you. My family arranged my marriage. We had been very rich but my papa died and left us in a lot of debt. The only choice my family had was for the eldest to get married.'

'Which was you?' said Taylor.

'Yes,' said Sabrina, 'so my family arranged for me to marry this man, who they thought was rich, but really he was just greedy and power-hungry. He thought we had money. That's all he wanted, my family's money, but little did he know we were all out.'

'So he killed you?' said Taylor.

'Not right away,' said Sabrina. 'We got married, and after the wedding I went straight to our hotel room to hide my necklace.

'Why?' said Taylor.

'It was a special necklace.' Sabrina sounded as though she might cry again. 'It was handed down from my Papa. He always wanted to see me wear it for my wedding, so I wore it for him, but when my new husband saw the necklace he started to ask questions about how much it was worth.'

'Did you tell him?' said Taylor.

'No,' said Sabrina. 'And he got so angry,' she sobbed, 'that's when he killed me. He strangled me. He choked me to death.'

'So why are you still here?' said Taylor. 'You said earlier

that you're not crossing over until he gets it. Do you mean the necklace?'

'Yes,' said Sabrina.

'But who?' said Taylor. 'Who do you want to get the necklace?'

'My great-grandnephew,' said Sabrina. 'He's the only one who is left on my side of the family and he's working here in this hotel. He knows about this room but he doesn't know about me or how I died. Do you think you could find him and tell him?'

'Yeah, sure,' said Taylor, 'but can you tell me where he is?'

'Well, I know he spends his time in this big office with lots of pictures of me and my family but that's all I know,' said Sabrina.

'OK,' Taylor said, looking at her watch. 'Well, it's too late now. We'll start tomorrow.'

The next day Taylor and Laura went down to the lobby.

'Hey! Look!' said Laura, pointing to a beautifully decorated room opposite the reception desk, filled with pictures of Sabrina and her family.

'Who do you think owns this office?' said Taylor.

'Looks like it's Mr Corvetti,' Laura pointed to a name tag on the desk.

'Isn't that the manager?' said Taylor.

'It certainly is,' said a voice behind them. It was Mr Corvetti. 'What are you doing in here, girls?' he said. 'This is a private room.'

'We wanted to ask you about Room 220.' Laura was shaking.

'Yes, what about it?' said Mr Corvetti.

'Did you know you had a relative called Sabrina?' said Taylor.

'Yes.' Mr Corvetti looked surprised. 'She's my great-grandaunt, but how do you know about her?'

'She's here,' said Taylor. 'She's still in the hotel. She has something for you and she can't cross over until she shows you.'

Mr Corvetti's face dropped.

'I knew she was still here,' he said. 'I feel her every time I walk into the room, but wait—what's crossing over?'

'It's when a spirit crosses over into the light,' said Taylor.

'The light?' said Mr Corvetti.

'It is like their piece of heaven,' said Taylor. 'Come on. Come up to Room 220 and we'll show you.'

Mr Corvetti, Taylor and Laura made their way up to Room 220. They pushed the door open.

'Sabrina?' said Taylor. 'Are you here?'

'Yes,' Sabrina replied, and suddenly Taylor could see her.

'We've found your nephew,' she said, 'Mr Corvetti.' She pointed at him. 'He's the Manager here.'

Sabrina nodded, smiling. She pointed to the floorboard where she had hidden the locket. Taylor knelt, then pulled up the floorboard to reveal the pretty, pale pink box. She handed it to Mr Corvetti whose face fell back in shock when he opened it and saw the locket.

'Sabrina wanted you to have this,' said Taylor.

Suddenly a bright light shone through the room.

'What is that?' Sabrina spoke to Taylor. 'It's so bright,' she said.

'It's the light,' said Taylor. 'Now you can go. You're ready.'

'Thank you so much, Taylor,' said Sabrina. 'I'll never forget you.' Her face looked like it was finally at peace.

Moving slowly, she drifted into the light, fading back, and then she was gone.

'Thank you girls,' said Mr Corvetti. 'You don't know how much this means to me.'

Taylor and Laura went back up to their room.

'Come on,' said Taylor. 'Let's go and enjoy the rest of the holiday.'

The last few days of the holiday went by like they were only a few minutes, and before they knew it the girls were in their room, packing to go home.

'What do you think our parents will say when we tell them about Sabrina?' said Taylor.

'I don't know. They probably won't believe us,' said Laura. 'Better hurry, we have to be at the airport in an hour.'

'OK. I'm packed,' said Taylor.

Just like before, the journey was long and boring but they soon made it home, where they each told their parents about the hotel and how it was haunted by the ghost of Sabrina. Laura was right. Their parents didn't believe a word.

'I told you they wouldn't believe us,' said Laura.

'Ah well,' said Taylor, 'at least we know we did something good for someone else, and we know Sabrina is happy.'

Dangerous Rumours
Jonathan Moore

The Start

It was when they had their small break in school that the gym window got smashed. They were playing football and somebody threw a stone. The minute it hit the window they heard a big smash. They turned around and there was a huge hole in the window. There was lots of glass everywhere. The rock had been thrown from inside the gym.

Kevin was outside the window. There were shards of glass in his arms as he'd been wearing a T-shirt. The rock had hit him in the back of the head and there was a huge gash under his hair.

The principal, Mr Mac, and the vice principal, Mr Byrne, charged out to the yard. Sean and his mates were standing near the window, and Mr Mac and Mr Byrne came over.

'Who smashed the window?' shouted Mr Mac.

'It wasn't me, so don't blame me,' Paul said.

'It definitely wasn't me because I was playing football,' Sean said.

'Two of you into my office now!' Mr Mac said angrily.

'You can't blame us two, we were playing football,' Sean said.

'UP TO THE OFFICE NOW!'

Paul and Sean strolled behind him. They were trying not to giggle.

'HURRY UP, YOU TWO!'

When they got to the office, Sean said to Paul: 'Who did it? Was it you?'

He started to get angry. 'It wasn't me,' he shouted.

'I was only asking you a question,' Sean said.

'Alri, I'm just a bit nervous,' Paul said.

The Office

Paul got called into the office first. Sean sat nervously. Paul came out with an angry face.

'What's wrong with you?' Sean asked.

'Nothing,' Paul replied.

Sean got called into the office next.

'You know that this is very serious matter, don't you?' Mr Mac said.

'Yeah.'

'I know you did it.'

'I didn't. I was playing football when I heard the noise.'

'It was either you or Paul.'

'It wasn't, Sir, cos we were playing football.'

'I'm going to find out who did it, and if it was you, you're going to be in serious trouble for lying, as well as costing the school money and a student has been injured.'

'I know, well it wasn't us two.'

The Detective

Then the principal went around to the classes and asked who had injured Kevin. Nobody said anything because they didn't want to be called a rat.

Soon Kevin was back in school and he was on a headhunt to see who had thrown the rock that bust his head open. He asked Sean first.

'Was that you who threw the rock?'

Kevin was a big chap but Sean was not scared of him.

'It wasn't me anyway cos I was playing football with all the lads,' Sean said.

'Well, if I find out it was you that bust me open I will break your jaw,' Kevin said.

Then Paul walked over to Sean and Kevin where they were talking.

Kevin said: 'Did you throw that rock?'

Paul: 'No, ask him, I was playing football with all of them as well.'

Kevin: 'Well, if I find out it was you, I'll break your legs.'

Paul looked at Sean. Then said: 'Alri then.'

'You won't go near him, yeh dope,' Sean said.

Kevin just said: 'We will see,' and walked away. Paul looked afraid when Kevin said he would break his legs because Paul was not a fighter.

The Eyewitness

Later that day an eyewitness named Ashleigh told Kevin, and most of all Mr Mac, that she saw Sean playing football the whole time. She only told because nobody else had the courage to tell. Then Mr Mac came into Sean's class and called him outside and apologised to Sean for accusing him of smashing the window.

Mr Mac: 'I had no right of accusing you with no proof.'

Sean: 'It's OK, Sir, but the next time will you not accuse me in the wrong if you don't know who it was?'

Mr Mac: 'OK, Sean.'

It felt good for Sean that his name was in the clear and he wasn't stressed anymore and most of all he didn't have Mr Mac thinking that he had done it.

The next day in school Sean went over to Ashleigh to thank her for clearing his name.

Ashleigh: 'No problem.'

Sean: 'What class are you in?'

'302. What about you?' Ashleigh said.

'305,' Sean said.

Ashleigh said: 'OK, I'll see you later.'

Sean said: 'Alri then, bye.'

Finding Out

After this, Sean went over to Paul and asked him if his name was in the clear.

Paul said, 'Yeah, Ashleigh told them that it wasn't me. How about you?'

Sean: 'Same, I'm delighted.'

Then Sean says, 'Who done it, do yeh know?'

Paul: 'It was Gav, out of first year.'

Sean: 'He's one of me best mates, I hope he didn't get caught. How did they find out?'

Paul says, 'Eh, there were just rumours going around the school and Mr Mac heard them.'

Sean: 'Okay then, I'll talk to yeh later.'

Then this conversation was over and Sean went over to Gav.

'What's up?' Sean said.

'Nothing really, you?' Gav said.

'Did you get caught for smashing that window?' Sean asked.

'Yeah, can't believe it!' Gav said.

'Are yeh melted mate?' Sean said.

'Yeah, me ma's gonna bate me,' Gav laughed.

'Will I knock for yeh later?' Sean said.

'Dunno, I'll prob be grounded, so ring me first,' Gav said.

'Alri then, I'll talk to yeh later,' Sean said.

The Build Up To The Fight

Then Sean saw Gav's ma in the school. She had to pay for the window and for the hospital bill for Kevin.

Word went around the school that Kevin and Gav had arranged a fight after school. Gav was big, but he was younger and didn't

go around starting fights or bullying people but he had a really bad temper. Kevin was a big nut, a hardman. He went around trying to bully people who were either younger or smaller than him.

At breaktime Sean went over to Gav and asked was it true that he was fighting Kevin.

'Yeah, but I'm still going to whip him around with the stick afterwards,' Gav said.

'OK, man, I'll be there so if anybody else jumps in I will jump in for yeh,' Sean said.

'Alri, pal, see you there then.'

Then Gav just walked away.

The Fight

It was a warm day and most of the people were from the school but there were some people that were in different schools because some of Kevin's and Gav's mates weren't in the school. It was in the park across the road from the school.

It started off by everybody making a circle around them. Sean looked over and saw Ashleigh gazing over at him. Kevin and Gav both took off their T-shirts because it was so warm. The two of them were stocky. They started off swinging and the crowd were cheering the two of them on. Gav ducked under a punch that would have surely knocked him out, but Gav caught Kevin with a lovely punch which knocked him to the ground and there was blood pouring out of Kevin's nose and his mouth. Then Gav ran for his stick and started to whip Kevin around with the stick. Kevin's friend jumped in so Sean went in too and started swinging digs. He caught Kevin's friend with one and it dropped him so he got on top of him and started loafing and punching the face off him. There was blood all over his face and also all over Sean's T-shirt. But then he looked over and Kevin had Gav on the ground and he saw a big gash on Gav's eye. Sean got a fright so he ran over and gave Kevin a kick in the face (blood sprayed everywhere) to get

Kevin off Gav. Then Kevin and his friends ran away because all of Gav's mates came up.

Aftermath

After this Gav and Kevin shook hands. But Gav needed to go to hospital to get stitches on his eye and Kevin had to go to hospital because he had a broken nose and he'd busted his head again. But everybody was all cool with each other now because the feud was over between Gav and Kevin.

The Ending

The school went back to normal again as there weren't rumours going around because the fighting was over and the rumours were about the fight. And Mr Mac wasn't looking for anybody because he already knew who had smashed the window which had caused the damage to the school and had also hurt Kevin. But the most important thing that made the school normal was that Gav and Kevin no longer wanted to kill each other. They'd shook hands and put everything that was done and said before behind them. It was a good school to be in now as there was no drama and no fighting or nothing like that.

A Trip Down Both Roads

Lorna Moran

Carla was brushing the floor in work when her phone rang. It was Cian.

'What's the story? What time do yeh finish work at?' Cian asked.

'Six o'clock, I think,' Carla said.

'OK, will yeh be out then?'

'Yeah, I'll knock for yeh.'

'Awri, see yeh later.'

Carla hung up and continued brushing the floor.

'Can you wash that lady's hair? Then you can go home,' Carla's boss, Sandra, said.

'Yeah, no problem,' Carla said.

She washed the woman's hair and then put on her coat. 'See yeh tomorrow, Sandra.'

'Bye,' Sandra said.

Carla rang Cian. 'Heya, are yeh coming into town?'

'Yeah, where're yeh?'

'Meet me at the Spire in ten minutes.'

'OK, bye.'

When Carla got to the Spire, Cian was already there.

'Heya,' she said. 'Are yeh buzzing into town till I get me stuff for that art project for Ms Murphy? It's due tomorrow.'

'Yeah,' he said. 'I have to get some stuff for it too.'

They walked up to Eason's on O'Connell Street and got

markers, rulers and an A4 pad each. They had a look in a few shops for their Christmas clothes too. Cian got jeans and a shirt and Carla got leggings and a long jumper.

The next day in school, Cian was acting a little strange with Carla. He wasn't talking to her as much as he usually did. Carla didn't know what was wrong with him. She thought maybe he was just tired.

When school was over, she went home and got changed for work.

Work was very quiet. She decided to text Cian while she was waiting on customers.

'Heya wats up are u coming into town wen I'm finish work?'

'Yeah,' Cian texted back.

'OK. I'll ring u wen I'm finish working, OK?'

But he didn't reply which was unusual.

A customer walked in.

'Carla, can you wash that lady's hair, put the towels in the machine and give the floor a quick sweep? Then you can go home,' Sandra said.

After work, Carla rang Cian. She told him to meet her outside the GPO. When she arrived, he was standing there. They went to River Island and got Carla's da's Christmas present. Then they walked back to Summerhill and sat on Carla's garden wall and talked for hours like they did everyday. Carla thought Cian looked unhappy.

'What's wrong?'

'Nothing,' he said. 'Let's go to the park.'

As they walked up to the park, Cian saw an old lady smoking. 'Have you got a smoke?' he said.

The lady gave him a smoke and a light.

'Thanks,' he said and walked away.

'Cian, what are yeh doing? You don't smoke,' Carla said.

'I felt stressed yesterday and the boys told me to take one and I did and I felt a lot better and calmer.'

'What boys?'

'Oh, I hang around with Peter and Josh now in school,' Cian said.

Carla knew that Peter and Josh were trouble so she didn't say anything else. She told Cian she had to go in for a shower. She was thinking about her best mate and the trouble he was going to get himself in by hanging around with Peter and Josh.

'Carla, come on down for your dinner,' Carla's ma shouted up the stairs, but Carla didn't want dinner because she felt sick over Cian.

In school the next day, she saw Cian with Peter and Josh. Peter and Josh called her a loner. Cian laughed although he felt bad for Carla who he'd known all his life.

'Shut up yous dopes,' Carla said, even though she was really upset. She walked up to her other friend, Chloe.

A week later, Carla spent her first weekend without Cian. She lay on her bed. Her ma came in and sat beside her.

'OK, what's up with you? You're not eating or anything. You're not yourself. You're not even out with Cian these days,' her ma said.

'Awh, go away, Ma. Cian has his own friends now,' Carla said.

'OK, we'll talk later. Get ready, you're going to be late for work,' her ma said.

Carla slowly strolled to work. Sandra talked to her about being twenty minutes late. Carla used the excuse, 'Me auntie drove me and the traffic was heavy.'

'OK,' Sandra said. 'Start washing that lady's hair.'

Carla started to wash the woman's hair.

'I don't want any conditioner please,' the woman said clearly.

But Carla wasn't concentrating. She picked up the bottle of soap and put it in the woman's hair by accident, then put a half bottle of conditioner in. She washed it out and turned off the tap.

The women felt her hair. 'But it's still greasy,' she said.

Carla wasn't listening. She picked up the sweeping brush and started sweeping the floor. She felt weak and dizzy and her

eyes went blurry. She sat down for a minute and started getting sick all over the floor. Everybody was looking at her. She was so embarrassed.

Sandra asked if she was OK and told her to go home. 'I don't know what's wrong with you; you're not yourself. You usually work hard and do your job well. You can take a few weeks off if you need to, but when you come back I want you working hard again, OK?'

'OK,' Carla said and left.

On her way home, she bumped into Cian. He looked terrible. He was falling all over the place and the smell of vodka off him was making her even sicker than she already was.

'Hey, Carla, yeh OK? Yeh've lost a lot of weight,' Cian said.

'Yep, I'm grand,' Carla said. She knew he was drunk but he was trying to hide it. 'How come I haven't seen yeh in school or anything the past few days?'

'Aww, I'm suspended for two weeks, did yeh not hear?' Cian laughed but Carla did not find it funny because Cian was usually real smart and quiet in school.

'No, for what?' Carla said.

'The other day, when you weren't in, the boys were all messing and Miss O'Connell walked in and they all blamed it on me and anyways she started roaring at me, so I pushed a chair at her and she thrown me out for two weeks.'

Carla wondered why he would be so stupid. 'OK, see yeh later,' she said. She went home and lay on her bed. Her little brother, Alex, came into her room and stood there, looking at her.

'Get out, Alex,' Carla cried.

Alex laughed. 'No,' he said. 'I seen Cian today. He was drinking and smoking. He looked like a drunkie.'

Alex ran out of her room and slammed the door behind him. Carla was even more upset. She rang Chloe and told her how she felt, but Chloe thought she was a weirdo and just said, 'Don't worry about him.'

Carla put on her coat and went to talk to her Auntie Jan. She

felt Jan was the only person who could understand her and make things better for her. She liked Jan because she was young—she was only twenty-two. Jan lived on her own with her four-year-old daughter, Amy.

Carla knocked at Jan's door.

'Where's Ciano?' Jan said, because she wasn't use to seeing Carla without Cian.

'Well, that's actually what I wanna talk to you about,' Carla said.

'OK, Carla tell me everything,' Jan said. 'I won't do what your ma does and tell Ciano's ma. I'll keep it between me and you, I promise.'

'OK, well I seen him, Peter, Josh and a few other fellas the other day down the lane beside Dunnes Stores smoking hash and drinking bottles of vodka and wine, and he looked filthy, like he hadn't slept in weeks and he asked me did I want some hash and I said no and walked past him. And Alex even called him a drunkie. He calls people who are drunk and take drugs a drunkie and he's only five. And Cian was doing really, really well on his football team. If yeh seen all the medals and trophies he won last year, you wouldn't believe it, and he let it all go for drink, smokes and worst off all, drugs. He doesn't even go training anymore,' Carla said as the tears rolled down her cheeks.

Jan made her a cup of tea. She put the cup of hot tea on the table in front of her and sat beside her. Carla went on talking. 'I can't believe it, all the times he told me how bad drugs were and how he would never in his life touch them. Like, we're friends since babies. I just want him to stop and be himself again but somehow I can't see that happening. I'm so worried about him. I can't eat or sleep. Oh God, he's gonna kill himself if he doesn't stop. I saw him the other day sleeping on the streets and he said his ma can't cope with him and told him to get out of the house till he sorts himself out. I told him he could come back and spend the night in my house where it's warm or he could stay there in the cold but he just said he was fine and went back asleep.'

'His ma and stepda must be really upset over him,' Jan said.

'Well, if I am, I can imagine how they feel,' Carla said.

Carla's phone rang. It was her ma.

'Heya, where are you?' her ma said. 'Cian's ma just rang me. Cian was really drunk and was stumbling across the M50 with them two boys he's been hanging around with from school, and he got knocked down. I don't know how he is but you might want to go up to the Mater and see him. He's in St Joseph's Ward.'

'Oh my God, are you for real? I'll go straight up now,' Carla cried. She hung up and told Jan. Jan said she would drop Carla up to the Mater and got her next-door neighbour to look after Amy.

When they got to the hospital, Carla couldn't believe it was Cian; he looked so bad. She rushed over to his bed. He was lying there with scars all over his face. His eyes were black and blue, his nose was bust, there was blood in his hair and on his jumper, and his trousers were all ripped. He had a broken arm and a fractured leg.

'Oh God, you look terrible,' Carla said.

'What happened?' Jan said.

Cian could barely talk, as he was still very drunk. 'I was drinking with the lads and I got a smack off a car. It was a taxi, a blue one I think.'

He asked Carla to go to the off licence and get him a bottle of vodka but Carla said no. He begged her but she thought it would just make him worse. He started getting sick. The nurse came in and gave him water. She said she couldn't give him tablets until the next morning because he still had alcohol in his system.

'Where are the boys now?' Carla asked.

'They ran off when it happened,' Cian said.

'Some friends they are,' Carla said.

Jan told Carla she had to get home to Amy and asked Cian if he needed any clothes out of his house, but he said all he needed was vodka or a smoke, so Jan just walked out.

After a while, Cian started to sober up. 'How was school?' he asked.

Carla talked to him for ages about school to try and keep his mind off the drink. Then everything went silent for a minute.

'I really wish I never started taking drugs or smoking because it's way too hard to stop, and I miss training and school and my ma. She didn't even come and visit me but I wouldn't blame her the way I am. I even miss going to town with you, and just chilling in the park, but I can't do that anymore without drinking,' Cian said.

Carla was happy to hear he wanted to change. 'Listen, Cian, if you want, I can ask Jan if yeh can stay with her till you're ready to apologise to your ma, and I'll even ask if I can stay with you, but it won't be easy at all.'

Cian was happy that someone could help him but not sure if he could do it. 'I don't think I'll be out of here for a couple of weeks so it gives me time to stay away from drink and drugs,' he said.

Carla rang Jan, and Jan said that whenever Cian got out, he could come up and stay in hers. She said her friend, Gerard, ran a project that helped people get off drugs.

It was getting late and visiting hours were almost over. Carla gave Cian a hug. 'Don't worry, we'll do our best to help you, but you're going to have to work with us on this,' she said.

'I know, I'll do my best,' Cian said.

The next morning, Carla had her breakfast. Her ma was delighted she was eating again. Carla called into Cian's ma to make sure she was alright and to tell her that Cian was going to try and get back to himself. Cian's ma said she might drop up to the hospital to see him later on that evening.

'I hope he is himself again for Christmas. It's only seven weeks away, not long at all,' she said.

'Don't worry, he will be. He's a smart fella,' Carla said.

She got the bus up to the Mater and bought Cian a bottle of 7Up and a roll in case he was hungry. On her way up the stairs, she saw Josh and Peter. Josh had a bottle of vodka in his hand and Peter had twenty John Player Blue. Carla walked straight past them and told the nurse on them before they got to the ward. They weren't allowed in. The nurse told them Cian could die if they gave him more drink but they laughed in her face and walked out.

As the days went on, Cian's injuries were getting better but he was finding it harder to do without drink, smokes or drugs. He was getting very sick but the nurse told him if he touched another drug or smoke he would be dead before long. His ma was going to visit him everyday, but she still didn't want him home till he was off drink, drugs and smokes. Three weeks later, he was allowed to leave hospital. His arm and leg were better but he still had cuts and bruises all over his body.

Jan picked him up and brought him to meet Gerard. Cian liked Gerard because he was young and had been through what Cian was going through. Afterwards, they drove to Jan's house and Cian asked Jan if she could get him back into school in a few days. Jan said, 'Yeah, no problem if that's what you want.'

Cian started going to the Kids Against Drugs project in Phibsboro with Gerard, and met some proper friends there who were just like him. He rang his football manager, Dave, and asked could he get back on the team. Dave said, 'Yeah, training next Monday.'

Cian started going to school again and two weeks before Christmas he was back at home with his family. His ma got Jan and Carla a thank you card and invited them in for dinner. She shared the news that she was having a new baby. Cian was happy he was going to have a baby brother or sister. During dinner, he got a text from Dave.

'Match on Saturday at five o'clock in the Tolka in Finglas. Do your best to be there.'

Cian was delighted. He told Carla he would never touch a drug in his life again after what he had been through. Then Carla's phone rang. It was Sandra, asking her if she could come back to work. Carla was happy because she missed work.

The next morning, Carla texted Cian from work, saying, 'Heya good luck with your match.'

'Thanks. Enjoy work and I'll see u later,' he replied.

One of Carla's customers was the woman whose hair she had washed the day she was sick. The woman looked scared but Carla brought her over to the sink and put a towel on her back so her jumper wouldn't get wet. 'Any conditioner?' she asked.

'Just a small bit, please,' the woman said.

Carla put shampoo and a small bit of conditioner in the woman's hair then washed it out.

'Clean the mirrors and the worktops, then you can go,' Sandra said.

Carla gave the mirrors and the worktops and the floor a good clean, put on her coat and walked home.

Breakfast
Dale Mulgrew

It was a warm winter morning, around 9.30 a.m. when the alarm clock went off. Sara woke up from her boyfriend's bed to turn off the alarm.

'Jimmy, Jimmy,' said Sara. 'Today is the day, Jimmy, wake up it's nearly time.'

Jimmy said groggily, 'Eh? What you on about? What day is it?'

'Just get up and get ready. Can you not remember the plan we made up last night?'

'What plan are you on about?' asked Jimmy.

'The plan we made up last night about the robbery in the Dunnes Stores at the Jervis that I worked in,' said Sara.

Jimmy replied, 'What can we do with the money that we get in the shop?'

'What you think, baby? We can go over to Spain and live and then we can have a baby and live our life in the sun,' Sara replied.

'Well, if we want to do that we better hurry because the store might close early,' said Jimmy happily.

'Oh hurry, hurry, get dressed, if we're late we won't be able to get the money to go to Spain,' said Sara excitedly.

They opened their wardrobes in silence and pulled out black bottoms and black tops. They both had black hats, but when they pulled them down over their faces, they turned into balaclavas.

Both Jimmy and Sara got dressed and were rushing down to

Jimmy's car. They got down the stairs, and Jimmy's ma said, 'Do yous want some breakfast?'

'No,' said Jimmy.

'Yes, would you please, I'm HUNGRY!' said Sara.

Jimmy in an angry voice: 'Come on! We're late. As it is you're the one that woke me up from a deep sleep.'

'Have no time now, in a rush. Hold me some. I'll come back in a bit,' Sara told Jimmy's ma.

Jimmy and Sara got into Jimmy's car. It was a black and white BMW 4.2 Diesel car with black tinted windows.

They took off from Finglas West. They drove down by the graveyard; straight down the canal, turned left and careened down by Mountjoy Square Park. They drove past Abbey Street, straight down the Quays, and turned right into Jervis Street Shopping Centre car park.

When they got into the car park, Jimmy said to Sara, 'You don't fire your gun. You're not trained. You'll probably shoot something or me. That's why I'm not putting any bullets in the gun, right?'

'What! And you're trained? Ha! Just because I'm a girl doesn't mean I can't shoot!' Sara said indignantly.

'I was in the army for two years but got turned out,' Jimmy reminded her angrily.

'I wonder why. You probably shot your sergeant!' replied Sara, laughing.

'Sara, just shut up!' Jimmy was furious.

They parked at Exit 19 just near the exit to Dunnes Stores in the shopping centre. Jimmy jumped out and checked all the tires on the car and checked if he needed petrol. He didn't. They were ready to go and do the mission they had been waiting for.

Jimmy told Sara to get out of the car. They both had a big bag and a gun each, but Sara had no bullets in her gun. They walked over to the exit point and Sara looked in the window and said to Jimmy, 'The coast is clear.'

Then Jimmy said to her, 'Get behind me now. Pull your hat down. We're going in.'

They went through the exit doors and all they could see were two sets of stairs: one for going up and the other for coming down.

'Sara, if the police come, this is the way you have to come up, the keys are in the car and I have a spare pair in me pocket so don't worry,' Jimmy said to Sara.

'Don't worry; the police won't come because we are going to do this the simple way and the quick way,' Sara assured him.

'Where is the room where the money is?' Jimmy asked Sara.

'Eh, it's down the back, take a turn and go into the security man and get the keys off him. Then go into the room two doors down from the security room,' Sara replied.

'OK, baby, don't worry; everything is going to be OK,' Jimmy told her.

They went through the revolving doors, pulled down their hats, ran past another set of doors and Jimmy roared, 'Get down on your hands and knees or I will shoot.'

'Oh yes he will,' Sara said forcefully.

'Shut up, you, and just stay there,' Jimmy said to her angrily.

Jimmy went down towards the back of the shop and turned left the way Sara told him to go. He saw the sign saying security box. He stood outside for a while and counted to ten, when he got to the last number, he ran in and shouted, 'Give me the keys of the room where the safe is because I want the money now and if you don't I'll shoot you.'

The security guard was so scared he just gave Jimmy the keys. He didn't want to be shot.

So Jimmy went into the room two doors away from the security box and he saw the safe. He went over, stood on a chair and got the safe from the top shelf and put it on the floor.

He put the key in and opened it. He saw piles and piles of money and was in shock. He couldn't move or say anything for some minutes.

'Rachel! Run down, quick!' Jimmy called.

That name meant Sara. She ran down in a hurry with the bag open.

'Hurry!' she cried, 'Put the money in the bag.' She checked her watch and shouted: 'We only have seven minutes left, hurry!'

So, with Sara's bag full and Jimmy's bag almost full, Sara said, 'Two minutes left—quick!'

They filled up both bags and were running out when Sara's gun fell. She started to run back for it, but Jimmy said, 'Leave it. It's fake.' They ran up the stairs, through the exit doors, and into Jimmy's car. They then took off in the car, the same way they came in.

When they got home they started talking about what they would do with the money.

'Go up to the attic and get the case,' Jimmy said to Sara.

Sara went up the stairs and pulled open the door. Jimmy was sneaking up behind Sara but Sara didn't know. She got into the attic and Jimmy ran up and double locked the door.

'I have the money. I'm going to Spain to enjoy myself,' Jimmy roared excitedly.

'That's not fair. Remember I helped you as well,' Sara cried out angrily.

'Ha! Ha! It was a fix. Plus, when you get out my ma has your breakfast for you,' Jimmy said, with an evil laugh.

Dark Days
Michael Murphy

Once upon a time in a little village called Arica, set in the high-peaked mountains covered in bright green trees, lived a wise old man called Otapa. He lived in this forest for many, many years, though he had grown up in a little city called Tranpi, where the fields were green and the birds flew high. He was separated from his family and the city when the war of the Northern Province was fought.

Otapa awoke from his afternoon sleep and walked over to the mirror to reflect on his past by looking at his scars. He remembered all of his past conflicts and pains just by coming across that one scar below his left eye. The scar was in the image of a half moon and reflected one of his worst nightmares. He remembered everything: who he had lost, who he had loved, and of course the awful Ruthar. Splashing water from the sink on his face he washed away all the painful memories to spawn a fresh bright day.

Otapa, leaving his hut just outside the village, bumped into Navaho.

'Good morning, Otapa,' shouted Navaho.

'It is a calm one indeed, young warrior.'

'You know I am older than that,' stated Navaho. 'Guess what time of year it is?'

'I try to forget it sometimes,' replied Otapa, with a sad, gloomy look on his face.

'Why would you forget the summer festival?'

'Ah, you speak of this summer's festival. I was thinking of this time four years ago when we struggled to get Ruthar out of these lands,' said Otapa, with a fake smile on his face.

'Well, he is gone now and it is the last we will ever see of him.'

'WAKE UP!' shouted Sheila. 'He's coming!'

'PANDORAAA!'

It had been five years since the girls had seen this dreadful nightmare and now they were faced again with the challenge of fleeing from the place they called home.

'What's happening? What's wrong Sheila?' questioned Pandora, just awake and lying on her perfectly stacked leaf-made bed.

'Ruthar is back, Pandora! We have to run, we aren't ready for this, not yet.'

Just at that moment a tree collapsed outside the hut they had built out of sticks, trees and leaves. Pandora rushed to grab her bags and sword, and fled through the escape hole in the back of the hut. They ran as fast as possible through the trees and woods: out through the green fields, past the swamp marshes, and into the mountain caves.

'I can't do this,' panted Pandora as she collapsed into Sheila's arms.

'You can, Pandora, just keep going. We are faster than him: he can't catch us if we run.'

'I'm finished running. It's been five years now and I'm sick of it. I'm not a coward, I've nothing left, he stripped everything I've got away from me,' cried Pandora.

Settling down after their talk, Sheila set out to find sleeping material and fire wood.

On Sheila's little walk she thought to herself: Will I ever see our mother and father again? Do they still remember me?

As she had these thoughts she flung a stick towards a tree, only to notice a dark figure just metres away. Staring for a moment at the mystic figure, she wondered if it was one of Ruthar's minions.

Or was it a spy who gave in to his terror? After collecting all that she needed in her sack, she decided to head back to the camp for some dinner and a good night's sleep. She spotted the figure again. Deciding not to take notice—as she thought it was just her mind playing tricks—she went back to camp.

Pandora had already set out the dishes of fish and carrots with hot milk, and had the cave sorted out for the beds to be set down. As Sheila set up the fire outside for dinner, Pandora asked 'Do you miss Mom and Dad? Do you think they will remember us?'

'I don't know, little sis. We have grown and new scars have been made, and old ones have disappeared. Let's just thank God we re-directed that horrible monster from the village,' replied Sheila.

Sheila woke up in the sunlit cave and heard the soft wind blowing in the trees and saw the birds soaring high in the sky. Then she saw an old man standing over her, looking down.

'Don't be afraid, child, I noticed you last night running past my hut, so I followed you to see what the problem was,' whispered Otapa, trying not to wake up Pandora.

'Who are you?' whispered Sheila hesitantly.

'I am Otapa, wise elder of the village Arica, in the mountains.'

'Oh my God, are your people OK? Did he come to your village?'

'What are you talking about, young child?' replied Otapa.

'Ruthar, the evil king, is back; he has been chasing us for days on end. He attacked our village long ago and nearly killed my whole family.'

'Calm down, my child, you and your sister are safe with me. We will go back to my village.'

Walking back to the village, Otapa was explaining the situation to Pandora, whilst Sheila walked behind them; she noticed a special tree—on one half it was green and the other half looked dead. Realising she'd wandered too far behind, she ran to catch up with her sister and Otapa.

As they entered the village of Arica there was a welcome from

Navaho who held out fresh new clothes and pointed out the hot water bunkers. As they washed up, Otapa and Navaho started talking about the girls.

'What happened, Otapa? Why were they running? How long will they be here? We have not enough resources, we must send out more hunting parties if so...' said Navaho.

'Navaho, I have some good news and bad news for you. The good news is that they are only staying for three days. No worries, you may eat your food as you wish. But the bad news is that he is back around our area. Those sounds you heard seven moons ago were not wolves or bears, but Ruthar himself,' replied Otapa.

'WHAT! What are we going to do? You know you're not strong enough to face this again, you saw what he did last time! We must pack up and flee. Go to our elders in the faraway mountains.'

'No we shall not, my friend, we shall stay and fight, for I have the new powers. It was not sheer luck I passed these two girls, but destiny. These two girls are the chosen ones—they were attacked by Ruthar when they were born and survived. Their whole village survived three attacks by this evil menace, and the third time it was these two girls who saved the village. We will all fight Ruthar together. That means you too, Navaho.'

Just as they finished their conversation Sheila walked up from the lake, which she had chosen to wash in over the hot water bunker made by the Arica clan. She saw Navaho walking down towards the lake. They met each other halfway towards the lake, but Navaho walked straight past her without looking at her. Sheila, slightly upset about this, walked up to Pandora who had finished her hot bunker bath some time before her. They sat down by the huge fire to have some nice food; roasted chicken and a cup of boiled leaf water.

Otapa stood up and explained the situation to the clan, and even to Sheila and Pandora. His next words were the words that shocked the whole clan and Pandora too, but for some reason not Sheila or Navaho.

'Ruthar is back around this region and we have but one choice left—we will kill him! Navaho, Sheila, Pandora and I will go find this beast. Tomorrow morning we leave.'

Shocked out of the heavens, Pandora still understood what the situation meant and she knew that fleeing was the last thing she wanted to do at this very moment, so she stood up and roared a call that inspired everyone to trust Otapa's thoughts.

Lying in bed later that night across the room from Pandora, Sheila was still wide awake. She wasn't able to sleep because of this burning feeling in her stomach. It had kept her tossing and turning and eventually she even fell out of the bed. She thought about mentioning her mother and father to Pandora again, knowing she would wake up when she began to talk, but just before she could mention a word Navaho entered the room.

'Hey, Sheila, are you OK tonight? I'm sorry about earlier, I was quite upset and Otapa had just told me your story,' said Navaho.

'Yes, I am fine, just upset that this all has happened. I'm sorry if I brought this terrible beast to your village. It was not intentional, we've tried to flee but he seems to find us a week later... no matter how far we run,' cried Sheila.

'My child, it is OK. You're safe here for now and that's what matters. I have heard Otapa mention you miss your mother and father. Are you OK?'

'Yes I am fine. I hope to see them when we finish all of this.'

'You will, my child.'

The next morning everyone woke up bright and early to pack the last of what they needed. Just as they were half way finished, a scout came running into the village roaring that the beast was near; he was just two villages over, maybe a day, two tops. So Otapa and Navaho stepped it up and got packed within thirty minutes.

The ride was claimed to be two days on horse and six by foot, but along the way they met men on horses (friends of Navaho) who agreed to switch horses, so they now had new, refreshed horses. After a day's ride, they suddenly came to a burning village. From a distance you could see that an army was forming to leave, though Otapa wondered, as this so-called army was less than a hundred men strong.

Galloping in on horses, the team of four rose their swords and roared as they clashed with the enemy, cutting and slicing through dead bodies, those revived from the dead, and even those who betrayed family, friends and their clans—those who are deemed dead from the second they leave the lands.

Sheila fought her heart out: slashing throats, shooting people in the face with her bow and arrow, even slicing off their heads. Otapa shuffled through men as if they were snow and he was a plough: he killed them even when he looked at them.

Otapa screamed at Sheila, 'Kill! Get inside and find out where Ruthar is!'

Just as Otapa said that, one of Ruthar's minions dug their knife right through his back going out right his front side. In shock, Sheila dropped her bow and arrow and ran for Otapa, slicing whatever came in her way. At one stage she was even punching everyone right in the face, because her sword was in the other hand.

She had jumped over bodies, kicked through minions and sliced right through the dead just to help Otapa. When she got there, she got her knife and stuck it straight through the minion's face; blood dripped off the sword onto Shelia's hand, though she did not move an inch until the goblin collapsed. As the goblin collapsed Sheila went towards Otapa to try to make him better, even though his wounds were outrageously deep and wide.

'Oh my God, Otapa are you alright? Please don't die on me, please don't!' shouted Sheila.

'My child, do not worry, for it is destiny. It was destiny when you met me and you are now destined to kill the monster behind those gates.'

As he said those words his body went limp and he was declared dead. Just as that happened, Navaho sliced off the last minion, only to see Otapa lying on the floor dead.

'It was his time, young one, let him pass. Say a prayer and let his spirit be free.'

Sheila then took Otapa's silver sword and stormed towards the village entrance, only to see in the distance Ruthar, and half a thousand dead minions lying behind him. They had all been killed off just before the whole village had been burnt.

Navaho and Pandora were sprinting behind Sheila, when suddenly ten feet ahead, Sheila was standing and another ten feet more was Ruthar, face to face. Everything went silent until Sheila shouted:

'You killed my friends, you terrorised my family, and put me on the run for years. YOU'RE GONNA PAY!'

Just as Sheila said that she sprinted forward towards Ruthar.

Football First?

Adrian Rafferty

Thomas Naysmith was a sixteen-year-old boy from Tallaght in Dublin and his life was football. He lived with his mother and his two younger sisters. His father was dead since he was a kid. His mother was kind of poor and had no choice but to work in a cleaning job at the local hospital. Thomas was really good to his mother and on the weekends he stayed in minding the kids instead of going out with his friends. His sisters' names were Stacey and Elizabeth. They were seven and eleven years old.

He loved playing football and it was always his dream to play professional football in England, so when a club like Coventry City came looking he was not going to turn it down. He accepted the contract and was told he was leaving at the end of the season. The season finished in May and he would go in July for pre-season training. He was really excited but did not want to leave his family. He always told his mother that when he became famous and had lots of money he would buy her the white BMW that she had always wanted. She drove a 1995 Nissan Micra and she hated it, but it was all she could afford.

It came closer to the time when he had to leave, and all he could think about was playing at the Ricoh Arena and training at the Ryton pitch everyday. Things just kept getting better for Thomas. He was going to Coventry. They had just been promoted. On the last day of the season they won the league thanks to two goals by Davenport, the club captain.

It came to the day. Naysmith left his family at the age of just sixteen and went to live in England. He was happy when he was told that the first thing he was going to be doing was flying off to Argentina with the first team for their pre-season tour.

On the plane Naysmith was starstruck because he was sitting beside all these football stars and he didn't know what to say to them. He really started to panic when Davenport came up to him and said, 'Alright, son?'

Naysmith answered quickly, 'Fine thanks.'

It took a long time for them to get to Argentina but it was worth it because he had just been told he was sharing a room with Davenport and he could not wait. For the next six days the boys worked really hard in training and in the friendlies they had. They were beaten in both games but that wasn't important. The manager of the club, Billy Davies, was really happy with the performance of the team. During the week Naysmith got quite close to Davenport while they stayed together.

On the last night Davenport asked Naysmith was it alright if some of the players came over for a few drinks in their room that night. It was Naysmith's first trip away so he wanted to stay away from trouble but at the same time he didn't want to sound like a spoilsport to the club's best player. So he just replied, 'Yeah, OK, fine, man.'

It came to around half eight that night and the other few players came over to their room. The players ordered alchohol and in the end the price of it came to over a thousand euro. The players started to get stuck into their drink and some started to get drunk but no one more so than Davenport. He was really the worst. He was falling around the room, spilling the beer that was in his hand.

Some of the players kept asking Naysmith to have a drink and he could not resist in the end. Davenport was slagging him because he wasn't drunk and accused him of being dry. Naysmith never used to drink at home so this was kind of his first experience. He got drunk fairly easily. There was a picture of Davenport's family on the locker in the room, and because Naysmith had gotten so drunk he accidently spilled a drink on top of Davenport's picture. Davenport ran towards Naysmith but the other players held him back. He screamed, 'What are you at? That's the picture of my family.'

'I'm sorry, mate, it was a mistake,' replied Naysmith.

'Yes, you will be sorry, you mug.'

The shouting and screaming continued. The players heard a loud knock on the door and didn't know what to think. They immediately thought they were caught. One of the players went to the door to open it and was horrified when it was the manager Billy Davies.

'What's going on here?' Mr Davies walked into the room. 'The smell of alchohol is terrible, everybody out now,' said the manager with his deep voice. All the players left except for Naysmith and Davenport.

'Naysmith, you stay in with one of the other boys tonight because I can't trust you two idiots together.'

The next morning all the players got woken up early and were told to meet in the conference room. By the time Davenport got down all the players were there and he walked into an awkward silence. The players heard noisy shoes banging off the wooden floor, coming towards them. They all sat up. They knew it was the manager.

Billy Davies came in and sat down in front of them. He had a sheet of paper that had five names on it. He called out the names and told the rest of the players to go to their rooms to pack up to go home. Unsurprisingly, the five players were the ones who were involved last night.

'So, lads?' said Billy, waiting on an answer but he got nothing. 'If you don't start talking now, you'll all regret it. I can make this much worse if I have to.'

Davenport was the one who decided to break the ice.

'Sorry, Gaffer, it was my fault, I asked young Naysmith here and the lads round for a few beers, and a stupid row broke out.'

'I'm really disapointed in you, Dav, I expected more from you.'

Davenport and Naysmith were looking down at the ground with their hands behind their backs.

'Right, lads, look, get the hell out of here now and don't breathe a word of this to anybody because if the press find out about it they will make it out to be more than what it really was.'

Davies was frustrated and kept flattening back his hair with his palm.

'But I have some bad news—yous are all getting docked a week's wages.'

A little sigh came from the players but Naysmith was happy because he felt that he got off easy. The players got up and walked out of the room but Davenport got called back in while the rest of the players kept on walking.

'Yes, sir?' said Davenport.

'I expected a lot more from you. You're the club captain, Dav, you should be preventing this, not starting it,' said the manager and then he told Davenport to leave. The players then all got packed up and left for the airport. The night before, Naysmith had forgot to put his phone on charge and his phone was going dead. He saw a call coming in from his mother and answered.

'Hello, Mum, how's things?'

'I'm sorry to say...' his mother began and then Naysmith heard his phone beeping and his phone went dead. He was really worried now about his mother. He wanted to know what was happening. He waited anxiously on the plane home to England and then he had to get another one to Ireland. He was just lucky the players got another break after that for two days so he could go to see what was going on.

He got to the airport in England and was told that the next flight to Ireland was an hour away. It was even worse because he couldn't ring his mother. He did not know her number and it was only in his phone. By the time he got to Dublin Airport it was the next day. It was 11.30 in the morning and they had flown all through the night from Argentina. He got home from the airport in a taxi and ran from the taxi to his front door and knocked really hard. His mother answered and gave him a big hug.

'Why did you hang up? I've been trying to ring you since,' his mother said.

'That doesn't matter, what's wrong?' replied Thomas.

His mother looked at the ground and said, 'It's your sister, she's been knocked down.'

'No way, where is she?' shouted Naysmith.

'She's down in the hospital—relax—she'll be fine, she's getting out tomorrow.'

'Come on, I need to see her.'

Naysmith and his sister Stacey ran from the house to the car while his mother walked slowly. Naysmith jumped into the passenger seat and his sister got into the back. When the car engine started the radio came on really loud. Naysmith snatched at it to turn it off because all he could think about was his sister. He could not wait to see her and see for himself how she was. He was so nervous.

They got to the hospital and his sister was awake and fine. He gave her a big kiss and a hug. He was really happy that she was OK. He couldn't believe that he had been worrying over a little fight in a hotel room when there were much more important things going on in the world.

From Ten To Zero

Sean Ray

My name is Paul Golden and this is my story. I'm sixteen and I am from Manchester in England. I have lots of friends and my favourite hobby is football.

My three best mates who I grew up with are: Peter Moore, Josh Dougley and Jonathan Mare, or Peanut. He's called Peanut because he's so big. We started selling drugs at the age of fourteen and fifteen. I was playing for a local team, but Manchester United scouts came and watched me play every week. I had been at United's Academy three times and I'd a good chance at making it pro. The day of my seventeenth birthday I got offered a contract for two years to play for United and get paid three hundred pounds a week. So I started cutting down on selling drugs when I got offered the contract, but I agreed to one more deal. Peanut didn't want me to do the last deal but Peter was very specific that he was making me do one more deal because I was in the gang for so long and I couldn't just walk away. Peter felt I owed him this last deal.

The day of the deal we were walking to meet the people when the police pulled up and asked us where we were going, so we all ran down the laneway and split up but none of us got far because the police helicopter found us hiding out in back gardens, then we got brought to the police station and got searched. So all the drugs we had on us were found. I got arrested for intent to supply and I could get up to eighteen months in prison, so my chance at football was ruined.

Manchester United would not sign me if I had a criminal record. I was so disappointed in myself and so was my family. I went to court and was sentenced to fifteen months in prison. The two of my mates, Peter and Josh, who got caught as well, only got six months each. I went into prison as a tough guy but as soon as I was in there I was put in my place when a guy came up and hit me a punch in the face and put a pen to my throat. It was the scariest moment of my life. Lucky the prison warden was there to help out. After that incident I dropped the 'tough guy' act and just acted as an 'ordinary criminal' in prison. In prison I worked in the kitchen washing dishes. I didn't like it at all.

While I was washing dishes I was thinking about how my life could have been as Manchester United's Number 10, but then I came back to reality as nobody's Number ZERO. Then I heard some lads talking about a prison football league and I knew that was my only chance to survive in this place.

So I took that chance and asked the warden could I go for the team trials and he said he didn't care, I could if I wanted to. I went to the trials with my cellmate Josef Frit and he told me he was a good goalkeeper. When we arrived on the pitch there were only twelve people there so we had a good chance of making it.

After the trials, the manager/prison warden told us who made it and I was picked in the team. I was delighted because now I had a pastime in this kip!

So me and Josef Frit a.k.a. 'Fritzy' went back to our cell and were talking about the team. I couldn't wait for training the next day but in the trials that day I found out how unfit I had gotten, so I made it my goal every night to do sit-ups, press-ups, pull-ups, just to get fit and build myself up. The manager said he had two months to assemble a team because that's when the first match was. Training lasted one hour and thirty minutes every day except Sundays because Sunday was visitors' day.

Every Sunday, my little brother Fred came to visit me and he told me about the week he had and about his football team, and every week I told him that this is not the life for him and he had to stick to football and stay out of trouble. Then Fred told me how my mum was doing at home and how everybody was on our road. I had been in prison two months and my bother Fred was the only person that visited me. I don't think my family wanted anything to do with me and that was very hard for me to cope with.

The next day at football training all we did was figure out where people played. We had twelve players in our squad and three quarters of them wanted to be strikers, but the manager picked where they played best.

After seeing my little brother and telling him to keep out of trouble I thought about myself and how I could get by in prison. I started talking to people about the football team and how we needed more players and I found out that there was a man in the prison who was great at football but didn't bother trying out for the team. So I went over to him and explained how we needed players and he agreed to play. I was delighted. He came to training the next day and we finally got our team sorted out. We started working on formations and strategy.

The day of the first match everybody was nervous but dying to play. We started off all over the place but as the game progressed so did we. After we scored our first goal we could not stop scoring. The final whistle blew and the game finished 7-0 to us. We were all so happy for a change. We were playing football and enjoying ourselves. After that, one match led to another and we were playing two to three games a week. And before I knew it the league was nearly over and I had served fourteen months of my fifteen-month sentence. The months flew past. The last match of the season we won 3-2 and we won the league. We were all so happy and I was the happiest of all as I was getting out of prison a week later.

After a few months out of prison my life was back on track. I got myself a job. Instead of playing football, I got my coaching badges. I am now managing my little brother's football team and I am back talking to my family. But I will never forget my experience in prison and how I could have been Manchester United's new Number 10.

Escape Me
Carina Tkachova

Monday

She was standing at the window. Sun tickled her face. She closed her eyes to try to forget but the sunlight on her face just made her want to cry. She opened the window to feel the sun and the early morning breeze.

'Nicola? How come you are up so early?' said her mother from behind her.

'Mum, I couldn't fall asleep all night and I am tired from trying to fall asleep.'

She started crying. Her mother's arms spread apart, welcoming her into their loving and safe warmth. They stood there for a while, feeling each other's hearts beating against each other's chests.

'I'll have to go to the bank today around one o'clock, so I'll go to sleep for now. Do you want me to give you some nerve-calming medicine?' her mother looked her in the eye.

'No, I'll just have a bit of breakfast and watch telly, OK?' Nicola attempted to smile but another tear came out.

'There are danishes on the table, and I got this gorgeous cheese and salami yesterday. Wake me up at ten, alright?'

Nicola walked into the kitchen and opened the fridge. Her decision stopped at milk.

'I guess that's the only thing that won't make me sick right now,' she thought while pouring milk into her mug.

A tear of milk poured down her cheek as she took a sip from the mug. Her hand then suddenly let it drop. The mug landed on the floor, smashing into parts. The sound of splashing milk echoed in her mind like rain. Shattered pieces of parted mug were flying across her eyes. She saw the image of it breaking and milk raining upon it like a waterfall playing over and over again, but every time the image changed a bit. Milk turned blood red. *Replay.* Pieces of mug turned into glass. *Flash.* Darkness played against the light across the beads of pearls, glass and blood. *Another flash.* A metal taste flickered through her mouth. Time trickled as the end came. Darkness covered her like a warm blanket. She loved the idea of calmness and warmth but the sudden stillness of time scared her.

Gasp. She caught the wall and leaned against it. She almost hit the floor. Her kitchen looked tiny after the magnificent nothingness came over her. She didn't know what had just happened. Blood was a sign of something bad. Suddenly it felt heavy and she wanted to let go of it as if it were a nightmare.

'This might be it,' she thought to herself. 'I heard about this kind of thing. Predictions, magic and the unexplainable. Visions. A witch.'

It all came down to keeping it to herself. Sometimes it is better to keep it all inside. Not to waste your thoughts on silly things—it is pointless.

Tuesday

This time you should take me away,
To a new place where we just might
Keep the night on the sky, eya-eya-ay.
This time we'll be crossing the lines
Turn you somewhere new,
Let's do it this time, this time!

DJ Antoine, 'This Time'

Oh, I wish you could really take me away, sexy. But I guess for that to happen I would have to get up… if you were real that is.

She took her phone from under her pillow and switched the alarm off. Eight o'clock. Sunny. Tired. Perfect conditions for the first day of the school year. So she rolled over to the other side and, hugging her pillow, promised herself: *Another ten minutes will be enough for me to wake up. I need to kill the time though.* Lately, she noticed, that when you think of something time stretches out. *Think about something good. A boy. A boy… what boy? A boy I like… hmm… who do I like? Alex? He hates me. Paul? No. Connor? Yes, Connor…*

Butterflies exploded into her stomach. They were flopping from her fingertips and thighs into her chest and neck. They tickled her senses with their soft wings and it felt like something was singing soundlessly inside of her.

'He is very good looking,' she moaned through a smile that was forcing itself onto her lips. 'Maybe he likes me?'

She remembered the feeling that appeared underneath her tongue. Pleasure shivered throughout her body, leaving warmth and excitement. She remembered all the times their hands touched by accident in the school corridor and all the times she caught him looking at her in music class. The look in his eyes was full of amazement and love but it was hidden behind fear and caution. She always had suspected that he fancied her but at times his behaviour proved her horribly wrong. She clicked open her phone. Ten past eight. Time to go.

As a tear of condensation rolled down the window, the bus stopped. She looked up to see who was getting on. A bunch of businessmen, a Polish couple, a boy. She stared at him. She knew him. Well, kind of. He got this bus last year as well. He was probably a year or two younger than her and he went to the all-boys' school not far away from her own school. He was pretty hot. You know this type of geeky fella who didn't even stand a chance of a girl like her fancying him, but she did.

He looked at her and gave a shy smile. She looked out of the window and smiled as well. He continued his way through the bus and, as there were very few seats left, he sat down beside her. Nicola pulled her bag off her lap and put it under the seat. He looked at her from the corner of his eye and did the same with his bag. He looked very nervous, she noticed, and she smiled.

He was so cute. She really wanted to talk to him but, somehow, she didn't have enough confidence, which was very unusual for her. It was very awkward as well. Too awkward. She just started laughing.

'What?' he looked at her with wide eyes.

'Nothing. It's just that we look so awkward right now!' she laughed back.

'Yeah, we do.' His eyes dropped down to his hands again.

'I don't know why I'm saying this, but, I really like you. For ages now,' she said, continuing to laugh. He looked very happy suddenly. He lifted up his face. Confidence lit his eyes and a smile played across his lips. He looked her in the eye.

'I like you as well. It is weird telling you this. Especially on the bus. Especially when I don't know you,' he said in a quiet voice.

'Can I have your number?' she asked.

'If you tell me your name first!' he teased her.

'It's Nicola, and can I have your name along with your number?'

'Yeah, sure,' he took out his phone and handed it over to Nicola. 'I'm Eric, by the way.'

They had the nicest conversation ever! He turned out to be fifteen. They were talking about so many things while walking to school and, when she thought it couldn't get any better, he hugged her and gave her a kiss on the lips as a goodbye.

Nicola arrived to school late. Only ten minutes late. She was so nervous! She felt like something important was going to happen today. She was walking through the corridor towards her classroom and she was shaking. Her hand lifted to knock on the door. Firm knock. She heard everyone go quiet on the other side of the door. Mr Brown called her in. She opened the door and her heart skipped a beat. There was Connor looking straight at her. Oh, and the only spare seat was nowhere but beside him.

'Nice to see you again, Ms Hassae. Being late on the first day back to school is not good. I hope you will be more organised throughout the year.' Mr Brown raised one eyebrow.

'I am sorry, sir. I will try not to be late again in future.' Nicola dropped her eyes, attempting to look as guilty as she could.

'I hope so. Now, sit down beside Mr Williams. I will pass down your book to you in a second,' Mr Brown pointed at the seat beside Connor.

'Hey! Didn't see you for a long time,' Connor whispered to Nicola, pushing a chair back for her to sit down.

'Thank you,' she said as she sat down. 'I know, it was a whole summer after all! You didn't change at all though,' she laughed.

'Nicola,' Mr Brown called out. 'Here is your book for this class. Please, try to focus on this class and not on Mr Williams.'

'Sorry sir,' said Nicola and opened her book at the front page to sign her name on it. A note landed right on her lap. She looked in the direction from which the note came and noticed a girl. Nicola turned back into her seat and unfolded the note.

Heyah babe! I missed yew so much! God, yew got tan! Wow…
Meet me before lunch at de lockers I hav so much to tell yew!
Lurve yew <luv> Luca xxxxx

Nicola finished reading the note and turned around to nod. Luca made big eyes and stuck her tongue out. Nicola choked on her laugh trying not to make any noise. She had missed Luca so much! Her best friend would be united with her again. It seemed to her back then that their friendship would last forever.

The bell rang. Everyone ran out of the class. Luca grabbed Nicola by her hand and squeezed her in a giant hug.

'God, I missed you so much!' Nicola kissed her on the cheek.

'Yeah, I know. I got back from my holidays only last night,' Luca made a sad cartoon face.

'So, tell me, what happened over the summer?'

'Ah, well, I met this boy over in Spain and... hey, are you alright?' Luca looked worried.

'God, I feel dizzy...' And she hit the floor, senseless.

Black. I am walking on air. I am in the middle of nothing. It feels so weird. A feeling of butterflies in my stomach tells me that this is déjà vu.

Suddenly, a loud sound echoed past her. She swirled around fast trying to catch the sound but it just disappeared into the darkness. Nicola tried to look up but she saw nothing. A sudden light that appeared from her right distracted her. She looked at it curiously but the intensity of the light blinded her. It appeared to get closer and closer. It moved towards her quite fast. Then, she realised it was a car. She took a few steps backwards and noticed another figure moving from behind. She wasn't alone here. She looked back and saw a bike and a familiar person on it. Nicola took another step back and the ground underneath her shook. She looked down. She was standing on some watery surface. A glance back brought back the memories. She remembered him.

'Connor! No, wait!' Nicola screamed.

As his name left her lips and echoed through the silence, everything moved really fast. An accident happened. Connor and the car collided and the colours blended into an image of horror on Luca's face hanging over her.

'Nicola? Are you alright? Nicola, can you hear me?' Luca cried out.

Nicola attempted to stand up but she fell back on the floor in mid-attempt. 'I have to help,' she mumbled as she tried to stand up again. 'Connor,' she called out again. 'I need to help.' She tried to walk forward but her feet would not listen to her; she had to hold on to a wall not to fall.

'Nicola, what are you talking about?' Luca got hold of her hand and tried to stop her.

'He went home early, he was sick remember?'

Nicola just pulled her hand away and ran. She ran for the door. She was stopped by Mr Brown. He grabbed her by her elbows and pulled her into his room.

'Nicola, please calm down!' He fought her into a seat. 'Now explain what happened?'

'Connor got into a car crash, I saw it. I just had a vision of it,' Nicola sobbed.

'A vision? Now, I assure you there is no such…'

'There is! I saw it all myself!' Nicola screamed through tears.

'Very well. I shall call the hospital to find out.'

Mr Brown dialed a number on his phone and waited. He then said something to the person on the other end of the line but Nicola didn't hear it. All she could think about was that flying image in front of her when Connor and the car collided.

Mr Brown put the phone down. 'He just came into hospital. He got hit by a car,' he said through his white lips. His face was expressionless.

They sat there in silence for what felt like hours.

'You shall be excused from school for the day,' Mr Brown broke the silence. 'Just one thing before you go, Ms Hassae. Don't go to the hospital today. Go tomorrow, OK? Because they will not let you in to see him anyway.'

'OK, sir.'

Wednesday

She got up early that morning. She had breakfast and got her books, only she wasn't going to school. She was ready to go to the hospital to see Connor.

Someone shook her. She opened her eyes and saw a middle-aged man looking at her.

'Sorry for waking you up, but you wanted to see Mr Williams

and he just woke up and is eating at the moment. You can go in to see him in around ten minutes.'

'OK, thank you,' she smiled sleepily at him.

Her hand reached into her pocket to fish some change out. She counted out a euro for her bus fare and stood up to go to the vending machine. A euro got her a drink and another two got her a sandwich. She had had no food for what seemed like days! As soon as the sandwich touched her tongue pleasure ran through her body. She gulped down the coke and it washed the taste of chicken and cheese away, leaving tickling sweetness in her mouth. She glanced at her watch. Fifteen minutes were gone.

She walked to the door numbered 634 and knocked on it. A 'Welcome' echoed from behind it. She pressed the handle and pushed the door open.

The room was very bright. And even though the blinds were up, all of the lights were on. A boy sat upon the bed with his back towards her, slouching forward. On his night table she noticed dirty dishes and a Daim bar wrapper. She smiled. As she took a step inside, he stretched his arms and his neck. He turned around. Emotions ran through his face and stopped at, what looked like, surprise. Or maybe it was happiness. Or a bit of both.

'Nicola?' He tried to stand up but pain ran through his face so he sat back onto his bed.

'Connor, I know how everything happened. Please listen to me.' She raised her voice because she saw he was going to interrupt her. 'I had a vision. In school, when you left.' She walked up to his bed and sat behind him.

They sat there in silence. He tried to understand the meaning of her words. It was hard. He didn't believe in this kind of thing. But why would she be lying? And how would she have known he was in hospital? Certainly, his maths teacher had known about it but he had said he would not spread the word. He did not understand. And the most mysterious thing of all was the fact that Nicola was sitting there with him, on his bed, and was worried about him. He was confused.

'I know it is hard to believe, but it's true. I didn't believe it myself at the start. Suddenly, I got very scared for you...' Nicola started crying.

Another eternity in silence. Nicola's breath was breaking under quiet sobs and Connor stared blankly out the window, thinking of what to say.

'I really like you,' he suddenly blurted out. His blank stare burned the window.

Nicola's sobs stopped and she looked up at the door. Could this really be happening? Her dream coming true? Her mind froze and a hollow shiver ran through her body, like a déjà vu of the vision in the kitchen. She shook it off and turned around.

'Connor?' She wiped a tear off her cheek.

'I wanted to tell you for years now but I was too afraid of... I don't even know what.'

'So what will we do now?'

'I don't know but all I want right now is to be with you.' He smiled.

She smiled to herself and moved her hand until it touched his. Her heart was racing against her chest as she looked up at him. She loved his face. Something deep inside felt a little out of place but she didn't care, she was almost happy.

'There is an all schools' ball on Friday in the Grand Hotel. Will you be my princess?' He held her hand to his lips and kissed it.

'Now and forever,' they laughed.

A kiss locked their happiness forever in that moment. At least that's what she wanted to believe.

Thursday

All week she was getting nervous about every single thing! Being patient was killing her. Every second passed like her sloweddown heartbeat. She could not wait to get out of this place. She was going to see Connor. He would be coming out of hospital tomorrow, they were going to the 'start of a new school year' dance together. But tonight she was going to a club with her best friend Luca. She was coming to Nicola's house after school so they could help each other get ready.

Just as she was imagining how she and Luca would go into the club hand-in-hand, her skirt pocket started vibrating. She looked up to see the teacher, who was busy enough explaining his scribbles on the board to someone in the back row not to notice her checking her phone. She took it out and hid it in the folds of her school jumper, just in case. She flicked her phone open to set a smile on her face. Luca had texted her.

Hey hun! Miss ya lyk hell): cnt wait till 2nait its gonna b gas! (;
I wil giv ya mii flower dress I kno yew luff mii xxx

So it was sorted then. She was going to wear Luca's flower dress. She didn't want to wear her own new dress because she was supposed to wear it to the dance on Friday. But what was Luca going to wear then? Luca was fast at texting back.

I'll wear mii birthday suit! :P going naked... Buzzin! Yew wil
c its beautiful xxx

She smiled to herself. Luca was always full of surprises. The bell rang its last voice.

Luca came after half an hour—she had got detention for not doing her homework.

'I am starving! I haven't eaten for a month or something.'

'Cheesy pasta and chicken will do the job, right?'

'I love you.' Luca gave her a kiss on the cheek. Luca's bag slid off her shoulder and fell to the floor with a loud noise. It seemed quite heavy.

'Is that your dress? Or is that just your make-up bag?' Nicola laughed.

'It's a dead body!' Luca made a scary face.

'I really hope it is not wearing the dress you promised to give me.'

'No,' Luca looked like she was thinking. 'But I think the reason why it's dead is because it choked on it, though,' she smiled wildly.

'You are not getting food now.'

'It's alright, I have so much chocolate that it would be enough to feed me for a year.' She stuck her tongue out.

'Hope you choke on it,' Nicola stuck her tongue back at her.

'Don't worry, I will.'

'Luca, hi.' Nicola's mother came in.

'Hi, Mrs Hassae. Nicola wouldn't give me dinner.'

'Bite her, it might encourage her to give you food.' Nicola's mother winked at Luca and disappeared behind the door.

'OK, I'll swap my dinner for the dress you promised me.'

'Deal!' answered Luca as the flower dress appeared out of her bag.

'And you will show me what you are wearing tonight!' insisted Nicola.

'This!' Luca said as a long satin yellow scarf slipped onto the floor from her bag.

'God, you were serious when you said that you are going naked!' Nicola freaked.

'No! It's a dress!' She started to take her jeans off to try it on.

Two minutes later, Luca turned around: the dress, that was the colour of the sun, looked amazing on her. It was like a beach tunic. It had a split across the shoulders and a golden belt around the waist. It was quite short. It suited her so much though.

'So how about we eat now?' Luca asked.

'Great idea!' Nicola smiled back.

They went to the living room where the table was full of food and lemonade. Luca looked so happy and jumped onto a chair and attacked the chicken. Nicola laughed at how silly Luca was and then, making the excuse of having to call Connor, she left the room.

Back in the kitchen, Nicola looked at the dress she was going to wear and shivered for no reason. She decided to try it on. She peeled her top and jeans off and threw the strapless black dress with big purple flowers blossoming on the fabric over her head. It looked lovely and made her look very skinny. Not like she wasn't skinny, she laughed at that thought.

'I wish Connor could see me.'

She danced too much. She was too happy to stop and it felt like the more she danced the more energy was flowing through her. It really felt like she was a part of one big world where everyone was happy and where your dreams came true. She jumped and kicked off deadly dance moves to the beat, screaming out lyrics as loud as she could, but the music was too loud and she could not even hear herself. Soon, her throat tickled with a light pain. She took Luca's hand and mimed some moves that meant going over to the bar and getting a drink. Luca nodded and dragged Nicola out of the pumping crowd.

'Get me one as well?' she said, handing her a tenner.

'Where are you going?' Nicola's hand stopped in mid-air between her and the barman.

'I am just going over to the girls to have a chat.' Luca started walking. 'It's been ages since I saw them!'

Nicola nodded and sat down. She took a sip from her glass and wrinkled her nose. Red Bull didn't cover the horrible taste of vodka. She took a look around. There were loads of people that were so much older than her. In fact, it surprised Nicola that the security had let them in because they were under age and looked pretty young. It would have been a problem if Luca's ex wasn't a computer geek because he had made fake IDs for them when Luca went out with him.

It took her another ten minutes to finish her drink and then she decided to go to the toilet. She told the barman to hold onto Luca's drink and started walking over to the toilet. She was starting to get a bit tipsy as she was extremely lightweight. For a moment she thought she saw her mother's friend, Rosie, so she jumped into the toilet doorway and, hiding behind the door, she peeked out to check was it really her. It turned out to be some other lady who, in fact, looked nothing like Rosie.

'She doesn't even have a clue about life. She is so stupid, like!' said a familiar voice from behind the double doors leading in to the toilets.

'She has no style, like! Why do you even hang around with her?' asked another disgusted voice.

'Because, she is the only person that is stupid enough to do everything I tell her to do!'

Loud laughter echoed around the glass room.

'And what are you planning to do about the fact that she is now with the fella you fancy?'

'I will steal him from her.'

'How will you do it, Luca?'

'I will make sure she is left out by everyone and turn people against her.'

Tears choked Nicola. Her throat hurt her even more. She swung the double doors open and held them open for a second. Luca's eyes stared back at her, full of surprise and hate. Nicola rushed over and raised her fist, ready for revenge over the one who had betrayed her but, suddenly she realised that this wasn't the way to sort it out. She just came up really close, face to face, and said: 'No wonder you are hated.' She held her middle finger up to Luca's face and said, 'Fuck you,' and then stormed out.

Everything was blurry and she could feel tears running down her face. She tried to walk really fast but the alcohol slowed her down. She took out the cloakroom ticket from her bra and got her jacket. She could already feel the cold autumn air as she walked down the front corridor. Someone called out her name. In horror she froze, thinking it is one of her dad's friends. Slowly, she turned around and was locked in a giant hug. She tried to shake the stranger off and look at his face. She was so taken aback by the surprise that she didn't even notice that he was kissing her.

It was Eric.

The next moment he was dragging her out of the club towards the park. She shivered a bit from the cold so he put his jacket over her shoulders. He stopped for a minute at the bus stop and lifted her chin up towards the light so he could see her face better. With the back of his sleeve he carefully wiped the running mascara from under her eyes and then kissed her forehead softly.

'What happened to you, my girl?' he asked in a sweet voice.

'My best friend betrayed me,' Nicola sobbed back at him sadly.

'Ah, you poor child.' He locked her in a hug.

'Eric, actually I am older than you.'

'I am so sorry, your highness. I will not say that ever again.' Eric smiled cheekily.

'I missed you so much!' She threw her arms around his neck.

'Really? You did?' His smile beamed with happiness. 'Well, if so, can I get you an ice cream and we will go to the park to look at the stars?'

'It is bleeding midnight! Where will you find ice cream?' Nicola laughed.

'Don't worry, I will. Just wait here,' and he ran back into the club. He came out a few minutes later holding two cones of ice cream and offered her one.

'So, we are going to the park?' she asked.

'Whatever you wish, my princess.'

Friday

She was in the hallway. Narrow walls. She could barely control her feelings and actions. She really could not control herself. Her face kept twitching and her hands were knuckled up so tight that her perfectly manicured nails were leaving blood marks on the inside of her palm. She closed her eyes once again, as if it hurt her to see, then suddenly opened them with the excitement of a child on Christmas morning. The image she saw did not change from what she had seen a minute ago, but it still made her gasp and smile a little more.

Her hair twisted up her head like ivy and, at times, it fell around her face, curling in spirals caught on a wind. Her dress hugged her chest tight, keeping it safe, wrapping her shoulders and trailing down from her hips to just over her knee. She looked beautiful. She knew that for sure but it was hard to realise it was her.

She turned from side to side to see how thin she looked.

'I am like a super model,' she laughed

She checked her phone for time. A text message from Connor got her hooked.

I cnt wait ta c yah! :) ily eva soo much xxx

She gave the mirror her best smile and, satisfied with what she saw, hugged the phone and spun herself in a dance. Closing her phone, Nicola checked her watch. It's show time babe!

The taxi stopped and she handed a twenty euro note to the driver. She opened her umbrella as she was getting out of the cab. The Grand Hotel really was huge. She could see Connor pacing back and forth while smoking nervously. He walked like one of his legs was still slightly hurting him.

She ran up the stairs towards him through the rain. He saw her and threw the cigarette away. He kissed her a long welcome and offered his hand to walk her in.

The inside of the hotel looked like a castle and she was a tiny princess at a ball. She glanced to her right where she saw her prince, faithfully serving any wish she might desire. She saw Eric waving sadly over at her; she had told him about Connor when he asked her to go to the ball with him. He had brought his sister instead.

She could see Luca giving her evil eyes from across the hall where she stood with a group of her other friends and their footballer dates. She felt sad and sorry for Luca. She knew that the poor girl was just too afraid to open up, so she hid under her spiky animal skin and bit everyone like a tigress. Nicola had tried to help her but it hadn't worked.

Then Nicola saw her classmates, who were waving for them to come over.

'Hey, baby, do you want to go over to them?' she asked Connor while pointing towards them.

Connor looked distracted by something and seemed not to be fully concentrating but he managed to throw a simple 'Why not?' to her. When they went over screaming began. Girls squeaked with excitement and fellas kept throwing meaningful *Oooohs* towards each other.

'I will go over to say hi to the others and I will get us a drink. OK, babe?' Connor kissed Nicola's forehead.

'Please don't take long.' She kissed him back on the lips.

She continued her conversation with her classmate, Laura, for another few minutes before she noticed a funny expression on Laura's face. She was looking curiously at what was going on on the stairs behind Nicola. So she turned around. To see Connor and Luca going up hand in hand. Smiling. Together.

Something pushed her and she moved fast through the crowd, following them and pretending not to hear Laura calling her back. She reached the bottom of the stairs as they disappeared around the top. She paused for a minute, thinking over if this was really the truth she wanted and if she was really ready for it. She decided on a simple *now or never*, and off she went.

Another double door in front of her. Just like yesterday. Another betrayal? Could she cope with it? The answer was the swing of the door. A beautiful scene of her best friend kissing her boyfriend opened in front of her. As the door banged against the wall, they parted and looked up, terrified. Connor pushed Luca away with the words, 'It was her,' while Luca slapped him for it and ran out screaming.

It was just the two of them now. She walked in. It was a huge library with loads of ancient books in it and a carpet that seemed to be a couple of hundred years old. Shelves spread across the walls and reached up to the ceiling. There were a few ladders to reach the top shelves as they seemed so high up. A huge dark window spread across the whole of the back wall. Connor stood with his back towards it.

She walked past him right up to the window and leaned her forehead against it to cool down a bit. He began to try to explain himself but she wasn't listening. She just stared into the darkness of the rain outside while counting the pearls that hung on her neck on a ribbon.

Then he tried to hug her. She pushed him off angrily. He started screaming. She turned around and told him to shut it. He tried to take hold of her but she slapped his hand off. Again. Then again. She tried to push away from him but there was nowhere to go. There was just the window behind her. She was pushing against it now. He tried to kiss her but she swung away from him. Her body smashed through the window.

Glass cut against her skin. She could feel blood on her lips. He tried to catch her and ripped her pearl necklace. Pearls fell everywhere along with glass and tiny drops of blood. She was falling through the rain and nobody could prevent that. Sudden fear of death rushed through her. Glass sliced her face and raindrops turned blood red when dripping from her face while she was in her fall into eternity.

The ground was close as she could hear the tingling sounds of glass, pearls and rain upon the pavement. Maybe someone screamed. Maybe it was herself. She smiled as she was looking at the stars while falling.

Then her neck cracked and her head seemed to explode. She closed her eyes to drown the tears of pain that she could feel coming. As the blackness of her closed eyes rolled over her she lost herself. She didn't feel the time or the rain. Blood seemed to stop streaming from her cuts. She stayed there for a while.

Then sounds started to come back to her. It was too loud and she wished she had stayed in the darkness. Something grabbed her wrist and squeezed it a little. A bright light shone into her right, then left eye. Her chest contracted suddenly under the pressure of something. If felt like someone was punching her.

'She doesn't have a pulse…'

'We are losing her…'

She fell through again.

Saturday

I got lost.

Sunday

Nicola opened her eyes. She saw a bit of light coming through the window blinds. She was alive. She tried to lift her arm up but she couldn't and it ached like a string pulling in her back. She tried to look around without moving. There were tubes coming out of her hands, chest and nose. Her hearing was starting to return. Some mad machine was beeping quietly and regularly. Yes, she was in the hospital. And that's when she noticed that there was someone snoring slightly beside her. The room seemed too small to have another patient in it. Nicola turned her head in the direction from where the sound was coming. The figure seemed to be sitting on a chair and was surrounded by flowers. It was too dark to see the figure's face but she knew it was someone special. The light from the window played against the darkness of the figure like a halo.

Nicola tried to call someone. She opened her mouth and squeezed all of her neck in an attempt to call out a name, but nothing but silence came out. She tried again and again, but silence remained. Her back and neck were killing her with pain, but she still kept on trying. Finally, when the pain took over her, her body shook in silent hysterics. She cried. She cried not because it hurt but because her happiness was literally in front of her but she was too helpless to reach it.

She cried and cried until her name broke the silent rule of her pain.

'Nicola?' a familiar voice called out. The voice seemed calm but she could taste the note of worry in it.

She opened her eyes and the room, blurry from her tears, stopped sharp at the face standing over her. He was perfect. Almost beautiful. She was waiting for him to come all this time while in the endless dream. He put his palm over her forehead and moved it back across her long hair as if patting her. They smiled. She tried to lift her arm up again to reach for his hand. As soon as their hands touched it all came back to her.

The pain, lost happiness, betrayal and her grand finale. Tears decided to play a second round on her face and sobs swallowed her smile. He rushed to calm her down and held her face in his hands.

'Nicola, please, calm down,' he whispered into her lips. 'It is all over now, you are safe.'

She took a deep breath and looked up at him. She was very scared to let go. He somehow seemed to realise that so he held tightly on to her hand and smiled widely. Suddenly, she felt sleepy and her eyes flopped closed. He kissed her forehead.

'I will be here. Now I will never leave you.'

'Thank you,' Nicola opened her eyes. 'I love you, Eric.'

She fell asleep.

I really wish that this story could have had a happy ending.

Nicola died on Friday the 4th of September 2009 after the accident occurred of her smashing through a window of the Grand Hotel and falling from a height of twenty metres onto the pavement below.

We will miss you.

For Asta

Luis's Football Life

Artur Vorobjov

Luis started playing football at seven years old; he liked football and played very well. By the age of seventeen he was playing for Newcastle, and now, at nineteen, this is the first big match of the season. He is playing well but his team is losing 1-0 after the first half against Tottenham. It's the FA Cup and Luis plays midfield. The second half starts and there is a free kick to Newcastle (seventy minutes in) because Gareth Bale handled the ball near the halfway line. After Daniel has kicked the ball, Luis runs up to the Tottenham penalty box; he has the ball and is left one-on-one with the goalkeeper. He moves towards the goalkeeper but, just then, the goalkeeper moves to take away the ball and he slides and kicks Luis's knee. Luis doesn't move, the medics run out onto the pitch and carefully lift Luis onto a stretcher and carry him off to the team hospital under the North Stand.

The medics examine Luis and see that the injury is very bad; the bone has come through the skin. Luis is taken to the hospital by an ambulance, where X-rays are taken of his broken leg. It's put in plaster and they give him pain killers. 'It will be a long time before I play football again,' thinks Luis.

Weeks later Luis is on crutches and is scared that he won't play football again. Instead, he stays at home and plays video games. His friend John buys him new games like 'Delta Force' because he's his best friend and wants him to forget the pain. Luis is very happy to get the games.

One day Luis goes to visit the team. His friend Karl, who wants a place on the team, asks, 'How are you feeling? Can you play next month?'

Luis says, 'Maybe I can play the next match, when they take this plaster off!'

'I'm sorry, I just found out the manager is dropping you from the team because you cannot play sooner,' says Karl.

Luis does not know what to say to Karl, he's just so very angry.

'Why are you saying this to me, dropped from the team? Why did the manager say nothing?' Luis demands. He's so angry he slams the door and goes home.

Next day Luis visits his best friend John and tells him he's been dropped from the team.

'For what?' John asks.

'I don't know,' Luis replies.

'You tried to call the manager?' John asks.

'Yeah, he doesn't answer. Listen, can you come with me tomorrow to the stadium?'

After a long pause, John says, 'I can't, I'm going to the cinema.'

'OK! I shall have to go alone then,' Luis exclaims.

The next day Luis plans to meet the manager, Mr Boyd, and after lunch Luis gets on his crutches to catch the bus to the training ground behind the stadium. He is tired by the time he reaches the stadium and he cannot find the trainer on the pitch. The team is training, practising their running and tackling. When Luis sees his old friends training, it makes him sad. He is angry that he can't find the manager so he goes home.

The next day, when training has finished, Luis asks the trainer where the manager is. The trainer says, 'He's on holiday. He'll be back in about three to seven days.'

'No!' replies Luis. 'Karl says I'm dropped from team. I called the manager and asked, "why did you drop me from the team? Can you call me back and give me an answer please."'

The next day Luis goes to the hospital and spends a very long time searching for the doctor. When he finds him, he asks: 'When can I have the plaster taken off?'

'I'll take the plaster off today,' replies the doctor.

'Great!' Luis exclaims, 'I've got the final coming up and I'm back at training next week.'

But the doctor shakes his head, 'You are not playing anything for at least another week. You can only do the gym, but no hard training for your leg!'

'What? But I've got to play the final real soon.'

'That's not my problem,' the doctor adds.

Luis feels he is fine and he's happy because the plaster has been taken off; but also sad because he doesn't have training for another week. He decides not to listen to what the doctor says and starts training harder: he cycles twenty miles and swims three miles and does this every day.

After five days he gets a call from the trainer, 'Hello Luis! It is the trainer. Can you come into training tomorrow?' he asks.

'Of course, I can come!' he shouts with pure joy.

There are four days left to the cup final. Luis goes to training and plays better than everyone. The manager is delighted with Luis because he is fully fit to play in the final. Luis tells Mr Boyd everything. The manager is shocked and decides to punish Karl for deceiving Luis. Karl is not allowed to go to the Newcastle and Everton final.

In the final, Newcastle win 2-1. Luis scores one of the goals. They win the cup and this is a day Luis will not forget.

A Fixed Life

Melissa Ward

'How can yeh say that?' Kellie said to her best mate, Ciara.

Ciara had told Kellie she wanted to run away because she wasn't happy living in her house.

'Don't be stupid, just stay in my house for a few days, like just for a break,' Kellie said.

'I can't do that on your ma. She won't want me causing problems in your house,' Ciara said.

'Ah, she won't mind. Go up and ask your ma can yeh stay in me house for a few days and I'll tell me ma you're staying here.'

'Alri,' Ciara said.

Kellie walked into the sitting room and sat beside her ma. 'Ma, can Ciara stay here for a few days because her ma and da keep fighting and she wants to run away an' all?'

'Yes, tell her to tell her ma she's staying here.'

'Thanks, Ma,' Kellie said.

Kellie walked over to Ciara's house.

'Hey,' Ciara said, and Kellie thought she sounded happy.

'Hey,' Kellie said back. 'Let's go for a walk in the park.'

The two girls went to the park. Ciara got talking to some fella called Stephen but everyone called him Steo. They were in the park for ages and Kellie wanted to go home but she couldn't leave Ciara on her own. Steo had been drinking alcohol all day and Ciara was telling him how low she felt because her family were falling apart. He offered her a can of drink and she took it to make herself feel better. Kellie had a bad feeling about him and knew there'd be trouble.

It was very late and dark and cold, and Ciara was locked. Kellie bumped into her friend, Wacker, and he helped bring Ciara back to the house.

Kellie's ma had been worried about the girls because they'd been out all day and Kellie's phone had been ringing out because she'd left it at home.

'What happened to Ciara?' she said. 'Where has she been drinking?'

'We were in the park and she got talking to some fella and he was giving her drink because she sounded very depressed,' Kellie said.

'Help her up to bed and we'll talk about it tomorrow,' Kellie's ma said.

Wacker was still standing at the door.

'Thanks for helping me home, Wacker,' Kellie said.

'Ah, no problem, don't worry bou' it,' Wacker said.

'OK, see ya tomorra,' Kellie said.

'Who's that, Kellie?' her ma asked.

'That's me mate, Wacker. He carried Ciara home from the park,' Kellie said.

'How old is he?'

'Seventeen.'

'OK, go to bed, Kellie. It's getting late.'

'OK, good night, Ma.'

The next morning, Kellie and Ciara were having breakfast and Kellie's ma came in and went over to the kettle to make tea.

'Morning, Ma,' Kellie said.

'Morning,' her ma said back in an angry voice.

Kellie said nothing and just looked at Ciara blankly. Ciara didn't know what to do or say. She was feeling very sick and ashamed at the same time. There was a knock at the door. Kellie slowly dragged herself up to answer it.

Ciara turned to Kellie's ma. 'Mary, I'm sorry for any trouble I caused last night. I don't know how to say how sorry I am. I know it was stupid of me to do that.'

Mary looked at her. 'I can't pretend you were an angel and you done nothing wrong. I'll have to tell your ma because if anything happened you, your ma would've held me responsible. I'm glad you realise what you done was wrong and I do accept your apology, but never take drink to impress a fella because it's not worth it. You should learn from your mistakes.'

'I know. I don't know what I was thinking. I was stressed and scared about what's going on at home and what will happen if me ma hurts me da when they're fighting an' all. I never meant to cause you to worry.'

'Ciara love, don't go anywhere. I'll be back down in a minute. I'm just going up to me room to get something,' Mary said.

'Alri,' Ciara said.

Kellie walked in and sat beside Ciara and just stayed quiet. Mary came back with a photograph of two young teenagers just like Kellie and Ciara.

'What's that?' Ciara said.

'That's me and my best childhood friend, Rosie,' Mary said.

'Oh God, is that Rosie the junkie?' the girls said at the same time.

'Yeah,' Mary said. 'She was my best friend until her ma died, and she took it so bad, she got really stressed and started smoking and drinking with girls and lads a lot older than her, and she left school, so me and Rosie stopped talking because I knew she was going down the wrong road being with them and I didn't want that for myself. Rosie thought it was helping her cope with the loss of her ma, but it was really making her worse. Every weekend she was drinking and smoking in parks and down lanes, and very soon it turned into every night of the week, then BANG she was addicted. She started to feel she needed it more than she wanted it. She was real pretty as a teenager. She had lovely white teeth an' all and now she has none and she's known as the biggest junkie in town.'

Ciara was so ashamed and embarrassed. 'Am I going to end up like that?' she said slowly.

'I forgot to tell yeh,' Kellie said. 'Wacker is at the door for yeh.'

'OK, I'll go and see what he wants,' Ciara said and walked out.

'Alri. What's the story, are yeh OK?' Wacker said.

'Yeah, I'm fine and thanks for helping me back to Kellie's gaff an' all,' Ciara said.

'Oh here, Steo was talking to me earlier. He was asking are you going drinking later,' Wacker said.

'No, I'm not, it's not worth it. I made a show of myself last night and I won't be doing it anymore. It's stupid. I mean it.'

'I was only messing, Ciara. I just wanted to see what you'd say. I have to go back up to me gaff. Tell Kellie I'm going and I'll talk to yeh later.'

'Alri, bye,' Ciara said.

Kellie and Mary had gone into the sitting room to watch TV. Ciara went back into the kitchen and had another look at the photograph on the table.

I don't want to end up like Rosie in five years, she thought. I'll never ever end up like her. I don't want to be like her.

Mary came in and saw Ciara looking at the photo.

'I'll never touch a drink again,' Ciara said.

'I know you won't,' Mary said. 'I'm glad you've realised you don't have to drink, smoke or take drugs for any fella. If he can't see you're worth more than a can of Budweiser then he's not worth it, is he? I don't want you texting that fella Steo anymore. I'm telling you for your own good.'

Later, Ciara sat at the table, texting Steo.

'Who you texting?' Kellie said.

'Steo,' Ciara replied.

Mary walked in.

'Give it to me now,' she said. 'I warned you.'

'Give you what?' Ciara said.

'Your phone. Don't be acting stupid, it doesn't suit you. I warned you not to be texting him.'

Ciara handed the phone to Mary. 'You can't take me phone for nothing. I can't live without it.'

'Well, you'll just have to deal with it. You were warned,' Mary said.

Ciara wanted to scream at the top of her voice but instead she sat there wondering: how will I get a new phone? Or if I'm nice will she give it back? Aww God, what if she goes through me messages and all me private stuff? What if she sees me messages I sent when I was drunk and reads them the wrong way and tells me ma and da?

'What if she doesn't give me my phone back?' Ciara said to Kellie.

'I'll give you a lend of a spare phone and we'll go to Meteor and you can get a replacement sim card,' Kellie said.

'Thanks Kel.'

'Do you need anything in town?' Kellie asked Mary.

'No, what are you going in for?'

'We're just dossing for something to do,' Kellie said.

'OK, fair enough,' Mary said.

The girls walked down through Ballybough. On their way, they saw Wacker.

'What's the story? Where yous off to?' Wacker said.

'Meteor. You coming in?' Kellie said.

'Yeah, I'll buzz in for a while.'

They walked up to the flats and saw Steo standing there. The smell of drink and smoke made Ciara sick.

'What's the story, babe, why didn't you text me back?' Steo said.

Ciara just gave him an awkward smile. 'Me phone's broke,' she said.

Ciara, Kellie and Wacker went into Meteor in the Ilac and got the replacement sim card. They talked as they walked up Mary Street. Kellie stopped outside NONAME. She'd seen a beautiful dress—a short, pink, strap-top dress with glitter on it.

'I might ask me ma can I get that,' she said to Ciara.

Wacker butted in. 'Mad Mary won't get you that. It's too short. It's only like a long top.'

'Shut up slagging her, you. She will get it for me,' Kellie laughed.

Ciara and Kellie bumped into their mate, Laura.

'Heya, I was gonna ring yous later and see if yous wanted to come to me eighteenth next Friday,' Laura said.

'Yeah, we will go. Ring me later and give me all the details,' Ciara said.

'Me too,' Kellie said.

'OK girls, I have to run. See yous later,' Laura said.

'You could've got that dress and worn it to Laura's eighteenth, Kel,' Ciara said.

Just then, Kellie's phone rang. It was Mary, saying that Ciara's ma had rung and Ciara's da was in hospital. Ciara felt weak with the worry. She had to sit down for a minute.

'What happened him?' she asked Kellie.

'He was just walking to the shop and he fainted,' Kellie said.

'I'm going, Kel. I don't know if I'll be back down later. I want to make sure me ma's OK and all,' Ciara cried.

'Do yeh want us to walk you up?' Wacker said.

'No, I'd rather be alone thanks,' Ciara said.

'He'll be grand,' Kellie said and gave Ciara a hug.

Ciara got to St James's Hospital and saw her da lying in the bed. He looked very pale and his skin was clammy.

'Da, you look terrible. How did this happen?'

'Well, I've been worried about you living in Kellie's house,' her da said. 'You shouldn't have to move out of your home over your parents fighting.'

'Listen, I'll come back home as soon as you're out, and look after you and help you get better,' Ciara said.

As time went by, Ciara's da was feeling better and he got out of hospital. Ciara told her ma she was coming home. Her ma was happy to hear it.

Ciara rang Kellie. 'Heya Kel, I'm moving back home cause I

want to look after me da. He's still not too well.'

'No problem,' Kellie said. 'When is Laura's eighteenth?'

'Friday. Are you allowed go?'

'Yeah, but I'm not drinking.'

'Me neither.'

'OK, talk to you later.'

Ciara was very happy to be back at home with her family, and there was no fighting. And Kellie was happy because her ma bought her the dress she wanted and new shoes to go with it.

The girls spent all Friday evening getting dressed for Laura's eighteenth.

Wacker knocked at the door. 'Swiss swoo girls, yous look stunning,' he said. He thought he was massive, standing there with his spikes in his hair, and his jeans and shirt.

They were all looking forward to the party. Ciara's phone rang.

'Where are yous?' Laura said.

'Just at the corner. See you in a minute,' Ciara said.

Kellie hoped nothing would go wrong and they'd all have a good night. They got to Laura's and Laura and loads of her friends were there. Everybody looked well. The music was pumping and they were all dancing. Ciara saw Steo stumbling over to her.

'Look what I have,' Steo said. He had a box of pills in his hand. 'Try some. They'll make you feel happier,' he said.

Ciara was tempted but she thought of what would happen to her friends and family if she took them, and she thought about poor Rosie.

'No, you keep them. I'm not going to end up like you, you're a loser,' she said.

And this was her new beginning.

Jocelyn
Cody Wheelock

It was my sixteenth birthday and me and my friends were in my room getting dressed and just having a laugh. They came around to give me my presents and we were planning a great night out. And luckily we were all in good humour.

Melissa is my best friend. We are friends since ages and we are more like sisters than friends. She's gorgeous—a blonde-haired, blue-eyed beauty—but with the loudest mouth I ever heard in me life. You'd hear her from here to Spain. Kirsty is me other good friend. She's the baby of the group. She's real quiet but when she's drinking she's a melter. Then there's Ciara. She's a real in-betweener. She talks to you and then about you, but besides that she's alright. Then there's Jocelyn. She's a big-mouth, always causing trouble she is, and nobody really likes her, but she'll always be with us because she's Ciara's cousin and Ciara wouldn't hear of us leaving her out. There's a lot of things I could say about my friends, but I'd be writing all day.

A normal Friday would be all the girls getting dressed in my house, two of us getting the drink, and then we would be just having a laugh, the way you can only be when you're with your friends—like ticks!—and all would be great until some certain person starts. Well, that was the usual before the Friday of my birthday. Suddenly the easy sixteen-year-old lifestyle got harder and it was like a bad dream with no chance of waking up. And every morning you would wake up and for a split second forget, and then it would come back, and so would the feelings.

On Friday we were getting dressed, me and Melissa waiting for the girls to come around from the off-licence, and we were planning on getting locked and staying in my house like nearly every birthday I had with them. Me ma was gone away and me Auntie Orlagh was minding us, but like every other twenty-one year old she loved her weekends so she was going out. She said: 'Do what you want, but if ya get caught I thought yous were gonna lie in bed and watch a film.'

Me: I hope Jocelyn doesn't cause trouble tonight. I'm not in the humour for her tonight.
Melissa: I know. I'll snap at her tonight if she plans on annoying me.

We were sitting there in the mirror when they knocked. Melissa went to answer the door.
Jocelyn: *(running up the stairs)* Yeh wanna see what's after happening! This dope at the Finglas bus stop goes, 'He'or, youngone, do ya remember me? 'Cause if ya don't ya remember me fella 'cause ya wer with em!' So I said 'No, I don't remember, but you'll remember me,' and I swung out of her. She was in an awful state, God love the poor creature.
Ciara: *(laughing)* It was gas!
Melissa: Yous would wanna give eh over, yez dopes.
Ciara: Ah, you relax, cryba.
Jocelyn: Anyways, are yez ready?
Melissa: Yeah. Wait for Kirsty first.

We waited half an hour and, after drinking all our bottles, started to walk down to Kirsty's. Ciara said she had rang her, and she'd said she wasn't in the humour but she'd come out for a little while because of my birthday an' all. We started to walk down by Railway Street, when Jocelyn said she'd remembered who that girl was, and she wasn't getting away with just a few clatters, watch what she was going to do!

Melissa: Are you for real, love? Eh, you're locked. Get her when you're alri in the morning.

Jocelyn: Shut your mouth, you. I'll do what I like, yeh tick.

A car pulled up beside Jocelyn and she recognised the young fella in it.

Jocelyn: Ah Jay! Haven't seen yeh in, like, years, pal! How's things? When did yeh get your car?

Jay: Well fleeced! Yeh coming on a spin with us?

Jocelyn: Eh, yeah, gowan since dese lil boring dopes aren't doing anything else.

Ciara: *(worried about her cousin)* Jocelyn, he's out of his head. I don't think yeh should go with him.

Jocelyn: Alri, see yeh after.

The car shot up the road like a bullet. I could hear Jocelyn laughing when it got to the corner. We were all worried but there was nothing else we could do. She's older, and wouldn't listen to us. Then a Garda car shot up after them. We knew she was in trouble.

We all walked back towards my house and we sat on the steps of the old houses. Ciara tried ringing Jocelyn's phone about sixty times. No answer. Everyone had told their mas and das they were staying in my house, so we were worried where Jocelyn would sleep. We started walking down by the bridge, when a fire brigade truck went by, and we were fearing the worst. A second later another Garda car flew past, followed by an ambulance. We started to run up to the top of the road. We saw loads of people at the top, and they were all being pushed back to leave a space. We kept running to the front of the crowd and then we saw it: the car upside down and the firemen cutting someone from the seat. I was right. I knew that someone was Jocelyn. People coming out of the pub across the road pushed past me, and I just stood there in shock and watched Jocelyn being put into the back of the ambulance. Ciara ran over to the paramedic and told him she was her cousin, and could she go with them to the hospital. He told her the police officer would bring us in his car, so we all got in the back and that was the start of one of the longest journeys of my life.

In the back of the car Ciara was like a baby, crying. 'I think I should ring my auntie and tell her what happened,' she said, but we all ignored her and just sat there looking out the window.

When we got to the hospital we were shown to a room and told we could use the phone that was there. Punching in the numbers was the hardest part of the night, and when her ma answered I couldn't get the words out of me mouth.

Jocelyn's Ma: Hello? Hello? Who's that?

Me: H-hello Anita, it's Sarah.

Anita: *(panicking)* Yes, yes love. What's wrong?

Me: Em, Jocelyn's been brought to the hospital, and she's very bad, I think. We're in the Mater.

Anita: O.M.G.

The phone went off, and I just sat there. I didn't know what to do. It was very hard. I rang me Auntie Orlagh, who was wondering where I was. She came up as quick as she could.

When Anita got there she was all over the place. She didn't know what to do. She was told to take a seat and someone would be out to talk to her in a minute.

She just looked at us and said, 'What happened?' It felt like we were to blame, and I felt real bad. We explained what had happened, admitted to everything—drinking, Jocelyn taking tablets and leaving with Jay—and she just looked at us in shock.

A nurse came in and asked us to leave. She wanted to talk to Anita, but she asked Orlagh to stay for support.

From outside the room we heard the screams and sobs from Anita, and the girls just broke down, but I didn't cry. I felt empty. There was nothing to come out. I felt I had to be strong for Anita, and not let her see me cry. When she came from the room Orlagh was holding her up and she was sobbing. Orlagh told us the doctor said Joc was gone into a coma, and that she was also pregnant.

Anita gave us a look to say, 'Did you know?' but we didn't. We were speechless. We had been like that most of the night. Soon a doctor came out and asked Anita did she want to see Jocelyn. She said yes, and we were brought up to see Jocelyn through a glass window in the intensive care ward.

It was weird, because in that bed was not our friend. That was the problem as I looked at her. She lay there with tubes coming from all over: her head, nose, arm, body—everywhere. Her head was swollen and her eyes were shut.

We left the room in shock. Orlagh said she would stay with Anita until her sister came, and we got a taxi home. It was getting bright out, and it was going to be a beautiful, sunny day in June, and everybody would be getting up and making trips to the beach, and the only trip we would be making was to the hospital.

After Jocelyn being in hospital for a while, things started to change. We didn't visit as much because we were getting fed up with going up and down. We stopped blaming ourselves, and started to blame Jocelyn for getting in the car and for going with Jay, for taking the tablets, and the bad decisions she made. And we hated her for pressuring us, for being the oldest and the example she gave, and for letting us believe she was right. But most of all we blamed her for the impact she had on Ciara's life, on everyone's life.

I sat at home one day, and was thinking how Anita had told us Jocelyn was well enough to come home, but was going to be living with her nanny in the country, and I was thinking I was glad she'd gone into a coma when she did—I know it sounds sick, but I was. Jocelyn's weekends were not enough for her anymore, neither were her drugs. She was ready to move on to bigger things that we were not able for, so in that way I was glad.

Four years later, I was on my way home from college when I saw a car pulling up outside Jocelyn's house. As I got nearer I saw Jocelyn being helped out of the car. It was weird, I hadn't seen her for ages, and it was mad looking at her. Everything was different. She hadn't got the sparkle she usually had. She was dull, and her lovely hair was cut short. I went to help but she didn't need any. I told her I would ring the girls and we would call around later, and she seemed happy. All the girls had drifted apart since the accident, and we barely saw each other anymore.

We went around. She was happy to see us, and welcomed us in. The house seemed real different, we weren't in it in ages. Joc just sat there and talked about hospital. Melissa brought my birthday up, and asked what I was doing. I said we were going out—me and Melissa—and Ciara said she was coming too. The smile dropped from Jocelyn's face, and she stared blankly out the window.

'We always had our birthdays together, didn't we?' said Jocelyn, 'and now I won't be able to go out with yous anymore, will I?'

Ciara changed the subject. We left soon after, promising to come back tomorrow.

Notes on the Authors

Desislava Baramova was born in Bulgaria in 1994. She lived in Italy for five years. Now she lives in the Docklands, Dublin. She likes shopping and music. She dislikes waking up early in the morning.

Dillon Burke was born in Dublin in 1994, where he lives in Cabra. He enjoys listening to music and watching horror movies, and dislikes spiders and snakes. He has two brothers, one older and one a twin, who is unidentical to Dillon. He also has a dog called Spike.

Graham Burke was born in Cabra in Dublin. He has two brothers. He likes watching telly, playing football and Playstation. He dislikes writing and school.

John Cooney lives in Cabra in Dublin. He was born in 1993.
Likes: football, music.
Dislikes: school, basketball.

 **Kevin Cooney** was born in 1993. He has family in Dublin and Liverpool. He is forced to support Liverpool Football Club. He likes sport and socialising. He dislikes school and when Liverpool lose.

 **Robert Courtney** was born in 1994 in the Coombe hospital. He lives in Crumlin, Dublin. He has a dog named Scrappy. His hobbies are football, GAA, and music. He dislikes insects and cleaning his room.

 **Josh Douglas** was born in 1994 and has lived in Finglas all his life. He enjoys listening to music, being with mates, eating from chippers and the summer. He dislikes the winter and fighting.

 **Carlos Donovan** was born in 1993 in Dublin. He now lives with his family in the city. He has a dog called Jack. He likes football, sleeping and eating. He dislikes ignorant people, cricket and greasy food.

 **Ashleigh Eyre** was born in Yorkshire in 1993. She moved to Dublin in 1996, where she lives now with her ma and her younger sister. She enjoys walking and going out. She has a few dislikes which involve school and men.

 **Rebecca Heary** was born in Dublin in 1994. She lives in Finglas with her family. She enjoys art, music and going out.

 **Kirsty Hogan** was born in Dublin in 1994. She grew up on Champions Avenue which is just off Sean McDermott Street in the city centre. She likes the weekends, because she doesn't have to get up for school, and she likes playing football. She lives with her family. She has three brothers and four sisters. She is the youngest.

 **Marian Ivanov** was born in Plevin, Bulgaria, in 1993. He moved to Ireland when he was seven and a half years old. He now lives on Hill Street, Dublin.
Likes: songwriting and having a laugh.
Dislikes: smokers and drunk people.

 **Natalina Marsella** was born on Dorset Street in 1994. She lives with her family on Dominick Street. She comes from an Italian family. She likes dancing, acting, swimming, boxing and going to the gym. She dislikes rude people and loves life.

 **Amanda Miller** was born in Dublin in 1993 and lives with her mam and two brothers. She likes to shop and hang out with her friends.

Jonathan Moore was born in 1994. He lives in Finglas. He likes playing football, sleeping, and going out with his mates. He dislikes getting up early. He has one brother and one sister.

Lorna Moran has lived in Dublin since she was born there in 1994. She lives with her Ma, Da, older brother and younger sister. She likes being with her friends and music.

Dale Mulgrew was born in 1994 in Dublin. He lives in Summerhill. He has two brothers and two sisters. He likes football, swimming and acting. He dislikes school, GAA and cricket.

Michael Murphy has three brothers and one sister. He likes rugby and animated designs as well as most arts. He is a computer nerd. He was born in Amsterdam in 1993. He is half Dutch.

Adrian Rafferty was born in Dublin in 1994. He likes sleeping and football and dislikes school and getting up early. He has one big sister.

Sean Ray was born in Tallaght in 1993. He likes football and swimming. He dislikes cricket and hurling.

Carina Tkachova was born in Latvia in 1993. She came to Ireland in 2006. Her family is too complicated to write down. She lives for fun and her friends, loves chocolate, parties, music and dancing. She hates crying, doing nothing, fighting and being helpless. She is a fashion freak and is too loud.

Artur Vorobjov was born in Tallin, in Estonia, in 1993. Now he lives in Charlestown, Dublin. He likes football and swimming. He dislikes Gaelic football and school.

Melissa Ward was born in Dublin in 1993. She lives in Finglas with her family. She likes music and going out with friends.

Cody Wheelock was born in Summerhill, Dublin, in 1994. She has two sisters and one brother and likes family, friends, and weekends. She dislikes girls smoking and rats.

Acknowledgements

The writers would like to thank:

Larkin: Máiread Byrne, Ingrid Fallon and Noel O'Brien;

Fighting Words: Sara Bennett, Claire Coughlan, Roddy Doyle, Emily Firetog, Katie Grant, Hugo Hamilton, Jean Hanney, Joanne Hayden, Caroline Heffernan, Michelle Laplante, Orla Lehane, Melatu Okorie, Daragh O'Toole, Adrienne Quinn, Vinnie Quinn, Jane Ruffino, Helen Seymour, Maria Tecce and Sarah Tully;

The Stinging Fly: Emily Firetog, Declan Meade and Sarah O'Connor.

*****

Larkin Community College is a co-educational college in the heart of Dublin city. www.larkincommunitycollege.ie

Fighting Words is a creative writing centre, established by Roddy Doyle and Sean Love. It opened in January 2009 and aims to help students of all ages to develop their writing skills and to explore their love of writing. It provides story-telling field trips for primary school groups, creative writing workshops for secondary students, and seminars, workshops and tutoring for adults. All tutoring is free. www.fightingwords.ie

The Stinging Fly Press was established in 2005 and operates in tandem with *The Stinging Fly* literary magazine as an outlet for the work of new and emerging writers. www.stingingfly.org

*****